FRIENDS
FOR
JOANNA

FRIENDS FOR JOANNA

ELISABETH BATT

LUTTERWORTH PRESS · LONDON

First Paperback edition 1971

ISBN 0 7188 1831 8

Copyright © 1964 Lutterworth Press

*Printed in Great Britain
by Fletcher & Son Ltd, Norwich*

CONTENTS

Chapter 1

LEFT OUT IN THE COLD

JOANNA stood among the Scotch firs at the top of the hill, and stared moodily across the little valley. Down the opposite slope her schoolfellows were tobogganning, most of them on tea-trays, two and sometimes three squeezing themselves on to one tray. But others had made themselves toboggans out of boxes and odds and ends of wood. Far and away the best of these was Heather's. . . . "It *would* be!" thought Joanna, smiling in spite of herself.

It was not that Heather Mitchell had more money than other people; she almost never had new clothes, and her family lived in one of the smallest and oldest houses in Hedley Green. But she was always full of brilliant ideas, and had the knack of thinking ahead. No one had been surprised to find that she and her little brother had a splendid home-made toboggan all ready for when the snow came.

Now she was dragging it up the track, pulling it to one side to avoid three tea-trays—each with two passengers on board—which came hurtling down, one after the other. Only one tray reached the bottom of the hill; the other two swerved, tipping their occupants into the snow where they rolled over and over, screaming with laughter. Now Heather was lending her toboggan to a group of small children who hadn't even a tea-tray between them. That was just like Heather . . . always giving things away, lending her possessions to all and sundry and forgetting who had borrowed them. She was always in trouble at school for losing her books and clothes, to say nothing of pens and pencils and indiarubbers.

With a sigh, Joanna turned away from the gay scene and limped down the hillside. The snow was no longer diamond-bright as it had been in the morning and at midday. It had that bluish tinge which comes in the late afternoon. It was tiring to walk through, with her thick-soled boot specially made so as to bring her right foot into line with the other. She need not have been walking by herself. Her mother had looked out an old tin tray and urged her to join the tobogganners, glad that at last there was an activity in which her child could take part. But Joanna had refused, almost rudely, saying she would rather go for a walk alone. She had set out in the opposite direction, but had come all the way round to climb the hill and tantalize herself by watching the fun the others were having.

Now she thrust her hand under her coat and up inside her jersey where she had hidden her sketch-book. She had kept it out of sight because her mother would have said that it was too cold to sit about drawing. But it only took Joanna a few minutes to make the little pencilled sketches of which her book was already half-full: a tree, a group of haystacks, a robin perched on a twig.

This afternoon she planned to add the old bridge

to her collection of sketches. The little stone arch, with the snow-covered banks on either side of the stream, would make a lovely picture. She found a tree-stump to sit on near the stream, and had brushed the snow from it when she discovered that her pencil was missing. It was a soft-leaded one which she kept especially for these quick sketches; and she distinctly remembered putting it into her coat pocket before she went out. She felt for it again. Yes! Just as she had feared, there was a hole in the pocket. Quite a tiny one . . . but big enough for her pencil to slip through. Her eyes filled with angry tears. She couldn't play games; she couldn't keep up with the other girls when they went for rambles; and now she couldn't even draw.

Suddenly, she wished she had gone tobogganning after all, even if only to please her mother. If only —if only she could get rid of the feeling that the others didn't want her—even when they had asked her to join them. If only she could be certain that they really wanted her; if Heather, for instance, were suddenly to stop in the middle of the fun and say: "Where's Joanna? Why isn't she here? Let's go and find her." And she would hear the crunch-crunch of footsteps in the snow . . . and voices calling her name.

It was a marvellous daydream . . . only, like most daydreams, too good to be true, of course. And yet she could almost imagine that she heard footsteps —on the other side of the hazel-copse. It wasn't imagination, either. Someone was coming this way . . . coming nearer. And then a boy, a boy of about her own age, came walking slowly round the edge of the copse.

His eyes were on the ground and he didn't see her until he was quite close. When he looked up, he took her pencil out of his pocket and held it out to her.

"Is this yours?" he asked. "I found it by the stile —at the bottom of Firtree Hill."

"Oh—thank you! Yes, it is mine," she said. "But—that was a long way back. However did you find me?" She felt sure she had never seen him before. He had light-brown hair and very "noticing" grey eyes . . . he was watching her face all the time she was talking. Yet he seemed to know his way about as if he belonged here.

"It was quite easy to find you," he replied. He had a queer flat voice, without any expression. "I tracked you through the snow. I couldn't go wrong . . . as one of your boots is bigger than the other."

He glanced down at her feet, and she felt her face flame.

"I don't wear it for fun!" she muttered, turning away. "If you want to know, my right leg is shorter than the left. And if you look again, you'll see that one of my shoulders is higher than the other, too."

She spoke bitterly, because he had sounded so casual about her wretched boot—as if it were quite an ordinary thing to wear. She had always thought that she hated people to feel sorry for her or to look embarrassed and pretend they hadn't noticed. But when this boy seemed to take it for granted, she felt offended.

Even now, he wasn't in the least sorry for her. He was looking at the stream and at the trees on the opposite bank as if she hadn't said anything. She scowled at him, until he turned towards her again.

"I'm sorry," he said then. "Did you say something to me? I can't understand you unless I'm watching, you see. I can only lip-read. I'm quite deaf."

Chapter 2

A NEW FRIEND

SHE stared at him in dismay. "D'you mean—you can't hear *anything*?" she asked, trying to form the words distinctly.

"I've never been able to hear anything." His sudden smile made her feel as if she were coming in to a warm fire on a cold day. "But you needn't look so sorry! I can't miss what I've never had. And you can talk quite naturally—so long as you look towards me. We all lip-read at my school; my mother has to remind me to talk out loud when I get home. At school, we don't bother to raise our voices."

His laugh was infectious, quite different from his flat, even voice. He spoke as if it was rather amusing to be stone deaf. Yet—it must be worse, far more out-of-things, than being lame and slightly crooked. For a moment she tried to imagine being deaf; living in a silent world, like watching a film when the sound-track has broken down.

"Don't you get—dreadfully lonely?" she asked timidly.

He shook his head. "Not really. I catch the bus every morning to go to school in Northminster; and there, we're all the same. And in the evenings, and at week-ends, there's the farm."

"Do you live on a farm?" she asked eagerly.

"We-ell, not exactly. It's quite a little house, about a mile from Hedley Green; but we've got a paddock at the back. Mum lets me have a farm there. At least, that's what *I* call it." He grinned cheerfully. "I don't suppose it's quite your idea of a farm!"

"I wish I could see it," she said wistfully. "It's what I've always longed for—to work on a farm."

"We'll go there now, if you like," he offered. "Only, first just let me look at these tracks down by the water's edge." His keen eyes were searching the snowy banks. Most of the stream was covered with a crust of ice, but this was broken in several places. One of these gaps in the ice was next to the bank; and on this part of the bank Joanna now saw scores of tiny marks in the snow.

"This is where they've been down to drink," he explained. "Look—this was a thrush." He picked up a stick and pointed to a trail of claw-prints. "You can tell it's a thrush, because they're in pairs; a thrush hops with his claws side by side, you see, while a blackbird generally runs. . . . That trail of big prints was a pigeon, I expect; and all these tiny ones were small birds, chaffinches perhaps. And look!" he shouted suddenly. "That's where a rat went down to drink. See the tiny feet and where his tail dragged in the snow behind."

"Here's something even smaller!" squealed Joanna. "Could it have been a mouse, d'you think?"

"No—yes—I'm not sure; I think it's . . . yes— it *is*! I really believe that was a weasel."

She had used her sketch-book to point with, and now he took it out of her hand.

"Can you draw?" he demanded. "Could you make drawings of these tracks—so that we could keep a sort of record of what we see?"

She was always shy when people wanted to look at her drawings, but she was pleased by his frank admiration.

"Joanna Wilson." He read her name on the cover. "How old are you?"

"Eleven and a bit. How old are you?"

He had to nudge her sometimes, as she would forget to look at him when she spoke. "Write down your age," he said. "I'm not sure if I've got it right."

Then he told her that he was twelve, and that his name was Andrew Fielding. He persuaded her to draw all the prints beside the stream, and the tracks of some rabbits near the copse, until she had made quite a varied collection. And all the time she was drawing, she was remembering his words—when he first looked at her sketch-book. He had said: "So that *we* could keep a sort of record of what we see." That meant that he expected to go on looking for tracks—together; that he intended to see her again. It meant that she had got a friend.

"I'm afraid we ought to go now," he said reluctantly, when she had finished sketching the big arrow-shaped prints of a pheasant, and the sweeping track of its long tail. "I expect you're getting cold; and I've all my animals to see to before dark. I'll show them to you, if you'd like to come."

He told her that it was just as quick for him to go through the village, so that they could stop at her house and ask her mother's permission. Joanna was relieved when he suggested this. She knew that her mother would soon be wondering where she was; but she had never made friends with a boy before—or with anyone, for that matter; and she had been afraid Andrew would think her fussy if she suggested going home first.

Mrs. Wilson had never seen Joanna look so happy and eager as when she flung open the door, crying, "Mummy—I may go and see Andrew's farm, mayn't I? It's only a mile . . . and I'll be back before dark."

"And I'll bring her home, Mrs. Wilson," Andrew said politely, standing in the doorway, as Joanna had not thought of asking him to come in.

"He's deaf, Mummy. He can't hear *anything*. So you have to talk so he can see your lips."

"That's no reason why you should leave him standing outside," Mrs. Wilson said smiling, as she beckoned Andrew into the sitting-room. "I'd like her to go with you," she told him. "But I'd be glad if you'd see her home—if it's really no trouble?"

She had heard of young Mrs. Fielding who lived at Stone House; that her husband was dead, and that she worked all day at her typewriter in order to support herself and her deaf son. Mrs. Wilson liked the look of Andrew. She would have let Joanna go with him even if his home had been much further away . . . if only to see the radiant look on a face which was so often sulky or depressed.

Andrew didn't start walking quickly, then suddenly slow down and suit his steps to Joanna's—as so many people did. He sauntered along as if hers was the pace he preferred and was accustomed to. She had plenty of time for thinking as they trudged along the side of the road. The wheel-marks of cars had made the snowy surface treacherous, and they had to keep their eyes on the road, which meant that they couldn't talk much. Thinking about Andrew, it struck her that his deafness had made him "noticing" in more ways than one. Not only had he learnt to observe the ways of birds and animals; he was observant of human beings, too.

Accustomed to studying their faces, noting their every change of expression, he knew just when a person was tired or cold, unhappy or embarrassed. He couldn't hear her voice or understand what she said—except by lip-reading; but she felt that already he knew more about her than other people did, who had known her all her life.

Chapter 3

STONE HOUSE

JOANNA had very little idea of how long it would take to cover a mile, and she looked expectantly at her companion every time they came to a row of council-houses or a group of cottages by the roadside. After a while, she nudged him. "How much further is it?" she asked, as he turned towards her.

"We'll soon be there," he assured her. "You're not tired, are you?"

"Not a bit. It's just that I want to see your house, and the farm. Is this it?" she asked eagerly, pointing at a very new-looking bungalow a little way ahead.

He laughed and shook his head. "It's called *Stone* House!" he said. "You'll see when we get there; it's not like any of these new, ugly houses. Here . . . this is where we turn off the main road."

He turned to the right, down a narrow lane where the snow was much deeper than on the main road. Scarlet rosehips gleamed in the hedges which grew on top of the snowy banks on either side.

"There's a farm—a *real* farm—at the end of the lane," Andrew told her. "But our house comes first. Here we are!"

The hedge on the right had given place to a low

17

stone wall enclosing a small garden; and from the little gate in the wall, a narrow path led to the prettiest house Joanna had ever seen. It was built of rough grey stone, and had two long, low windows downstairs and two smaller ones above. Creepers climbed the walls on each side of the white-painted door. Light glowed from one of the downstairs windows; and as they walked up the path to the door, Joanna could hear the clackety-clack of a typewriter.

"I expect Mum's still working," Andrew said, opening the door. "We'll just look in and tell her we're here; then I'll take you out to the animals."

There was a door on either side of the hall— which was really a short passage ending in a narrow staircase. The door on their left was ajar, and Joanna had time to glimpse a cheerful wood fire and a bowl of pink hyacinths just coming into flower, before Andrew pushed the door wide, saying: "I've brought Joanna to see the farm, Mum."

"I'm so glad." Mrs. Fielding got up from the table and took both the girl's hands in her own. She did not appear to notice the thick boot, but looked straight into Joanna's brown eyes as if she wanted to get to know her.

"It will be so nice for Andrew," she continued. "Living outside the village, and going to a different school, he hasn't got to know any of the children here."

"You ought to see her sketches, Mum," Andrew put in. "She's been drawing birds' and animals' tracks in the snow. We're going to make a collection of them . . . a sort of story in pictures."

Joanna clasped her hands tightly round the sketch-book; and, seeing her embarrassment, Mrs. Fielding suggested that they ought to lose no time in inspecting the farm before the light began to go.

"But you'll have tea with us, won't you?" she added. "I'll have it ready by the time Andrew has shown you round."

"The thing is, Mum, I promised I'd take her home after she's seen the farm," Andrew said. "And I think her mother wanted her to get back before dark. It seems a shame she shouldn't stay for tea, though."

Mrs. Fielding pondered this for a minute or two. Watching her, Joanna thought how young she looked to be Andrew's mother . . . in spite of the grey in her short curly hair.

"You're not on the telephone, are you?" Mrs. Fielding asked suddenly.

"I'm afraid not," Joanna replied.

"Neither are we. But I can use the one at the farm down the road . . . if there is anyone near your house who would take a message?"

"Mr. Pentney is on the phone . . . and he's only a few doors away from us," Joanna told her. "He never minds taking messages."

"Then I'll run down to the farm and see if I can get in touch with your mother," Mrs. Fielding decided.

So Andrew took Joanna through the kitchen, which was on the opposite side of the passage;

through a little wash-house, and out of the back
door which opened on to a vegetable plot with a
fenced orchard beyond. By a gate in the orchard
fence they entered the paddock, which was where
Andrew had his farm.

To Joanna, the farm was like a dream come true.
It was what she had always longed for; small
enough to look after without grown-up help, and
yet a *real* farm. There were two goats, Milly and
Mandy, each tethered by a long chain to a post
driven into the ground. In a home-made sty were
three pigs, which Andrew immediately let out for
their evening run; a large wire-netting enclosure
contained twelve hens and a haughty-looking cock;
while ducks, geese and bantams were allowed to
roam the paddock during the daytime. Andrew
had brought buckets of food from the wash-house,
and quickly fed the free-range poultry who now
had to be persuaded to enter their respective houses.
Then, with Joanna's help, he fed the hens and pigs
with a mixture of kitchen-waste and meal; and,
when all the rest were safely shut in, he led Milly
into a shed in the corner of the paddock. Having
tied her up, he fetched a small-sized pail and a
home-made stool, and proceeded to milk her, first
giving her a tin of bran to keep her quiet.

"Oh—*do* let me! Couldn't I try?" cried Joanna.
All her life she had wanted to learn to milk; and
this looked so easy and so much quicker than milking a cow—which has four teats whereas a goat only
has two. She had to nudge Andrew and repeat her

question, having forgotten that he couldn't hear her.

"I'd rather you waited till we start on Mandy," he said. "Milly can be awfully stupid and nervous with somebody she doesn't know. But Mandy's a good quiet old thing, and never kicks or holds her milk back."

He asked Joanna to fetch Mandy's bran from the wash-house so as to save time. While she was getting it, Mrs. Fielding came out to the wash-house and told her that she had been able to get through to Mr. Pentney.

"He very kindly fetched your mother to talk to me," she said. "And it's quite all right for you to stay to tea. I told her I'd walk back with you afterwards."

"How lovely! But—isn't that an awful lot of trouble for you?" Joanna asked.

"Not a bit. I'll be glad of the walk, after sitting at that typewriter all afternoon. Andrew and I will both come with you; and it will be a chance for me to meet your parents."

Andrew was leading the other goat into the shed when Joanna got back to him. Mandy was a silvery-grey colour, while Milly was light-brown with dark tips to her ears. Joanna thought Milly was far the prettier of the two; but Mandy was certainly very quiet and placid when Joanna made her first attempt at milking. Andrew started her off, and when the milk was coming freely, let Joanna take his place on the stool while he leaned over and guided her hands with his own.

"Gently!" he cautioned. "Pull gently but firmly, with a little squeeze; and try to make regular movements."

It was not nearly so easy as it had looked; sometimes no milk came at all . . . then it squirted in the wrong direction, missing the pail altogether.

"You're getting the hang of it," Andrew encouraged her. "Better let me finish her off, though. Otherwise it'll be too dark to find the eggs."

When the door of the shed had been securely shut on the goats, he stood the pail of milk in the snow, and said that they now had only one job to do. "I like collecting the eggs best . . . so I always leave it to the last!" he said. They lifted the lid of the row of straw-filled nestboxes at the back of the henhouse, and found seven eggs—four brown, two white and one speckled—which they placed carefully in one of the empy food-buckets.

"Now for the bantams," Andrew said, and led the way to a heap of straw behind the goat-shed. "They almost always lay here," he explained; and from a cosy hollow in the straw, they collected two more eggs—about half the size of hens' eggs. They piled the various food-containers into one empty bucket and Joanna carried them to the house, while Andrew took charge of the milk-pail and the bucket of eggs. In the wash-house, he poured the milk into a shallow pan and washed out the pail with boiling water from the kitchen. Meanwhile Joanna had been arranging the eggs in a wooden egg rack; but Andrew took the two bantams' eggs from her, saying that he was going to boil them for their tea.

Both were extremely grubby after their work, and Mrs. Fielding sent them upstairs to wash their hands in the bathroom while she finished getting the tea ready. They had it in the kitchen; boiled eggs, brown bread and butter, scones, honey, and a delicious chocolate cake. At home, Joanna never had much appetite and her mother was always urging her to eat more. But this evening she needed no urging to help Andrew to do justice to the spread. When at last they both had to admit that they could eat no more, they washed up the tea-things; and then it was time for Joanna to go home.

Chapter 4

A WALK BY TORCHLIGHT

IT was the first time she had ever been out after dark; and this walk by torchlight through the snow made an exciting finish to a wonderful day. She and Andrew took turns in carrying Mrs. Fielding's torch. When Andrew had it, he kept turning the light on to the bank by the roadside, pursuing his favourite hobby of looking for the tracks of birds and beasts. His mother had to keep reminding him to direct the beam of light on the road ahead of them, so that they could see where they were going. She did this by touch-signs; it was no use talking to him as he could not lip-read in the dark.

"This road seems so strange, at night," Joanna remarked. "I suppose it's because we're used to seeing a long distance ahead; and the torchlight only shows the next little bit of the way."

"Do you know that verse from the 119th psalm?" Mrs. Fielding asked. " 'Thy Word is a lamp unto my feet and a light unto my path.' I often think of that when I have to use a torch."

"I don't think I know that psalm," Joanna confessed. "When I used to go to Sunday School, we began learning 'The Lord is my Shepherd'."

"Oh? So there *is* a Sunday School in Hedley

Green!" exclaimed Andrew's mother. "I've been making inquiries, because I wanted Andrew to go to one. He lip-reads so well now, it's quite time he joined one."

"We don't have one now because Mrs. Gore is ill," Joanna told her. "She was the only teacher; and when she had to give up, there didn't seem to be anyone else to carry on."

Mrs. Fielding said nothing in reply to this; and after a while, Joanna asked her to say again the verse about "A lamp unto my feet".

" 'Thy Word is a lamp unto my feet and a light unto my path.' I think it is meant to teach us that, if we trust in our heavenly Father, He will always show us what He wants us to do *now* . . . the next little bit of the way, in fact; just as this torch lights up the next few steps. It doesn't cast a beam the whole way to your house; and neither does God floodlight the whole of our future."

"I wish He did . . . floodlight the future, I mean," Joanna said shyly. "I find it so hard to understand about—about God, and about what He wants me to do." It was the first time she had ever heard anyone talk about God in an "ordinary" voice, as if it were quite a natural thing to do.

"I think the great thing to remember is that He knows what is best for us. And if He gives us just enough light, that is, enough help and guidance, for a little way at a time, He must have a good reason for doing so. It may be because, if He showed us the whole way at once, silly and conceited people might try to manage without Him.

And then they would certainly come to grief! But in *this* way, we have to keep turning to Him to show us the next step; and so we go through life 'walking with God', as He means us to do."

They were now approaching the village, and Joanna took the torch and led the way to the row of council-houses, one of which—Number Three—was her home. Her mother must have been watching from the window, because she opened the door for them before they reached it. When they went inside, her father put down his newspaper and got up to shake hands with Mrs. Fielding and Andrew. While Joanna was showing Andrew her books and other treasures upstairs, the two mothers sat chatting together by the fire.

"I am so grateful to you for letting us keep Joanna for tea," Andrew's mother said, when Mrs. Wilson tried to thank her. "Andrew seldom has anyone to play with on Saturdays; and he does need companions of his own age."

"That's just the trouble here!" Mrs. Wilson said, lowering her voice. "Of course we know that Joanna can't take part in all the games and gymnastics at school; but she could join in with the other children far more than she does. She is so touchy and sensitive, though; and she has made up her mind that the others don't want her. She never seems to have any friends."

Mrs. Fielding looked disappointed. "I was hoping she might help Andrew to get to know some of her schoolfellows," she said. "She seemed so natural and cheerful when she was at our house today."

"May be things will be different, now she has got to know your boy. I've noticed a change in her, already," said Joanna's mother. This discussion was brought to an end by the entrance of the two children. But before leaving, Mrs. Fielding again brought up the subject of Sunday School.

"I used to teach in a Sunday School before we came to live here," she said. "I wouldn't mind trying to start a class going, if the Rector agrees to it . . . and if you think the children would come to it?"

"I'll come!" Joanna said, so promptly that both her parents glanced at her in surprise.

"And you'll be able to rope in some of the others," Andrew told her. "Enough to make a start, anyway."

"I'm sure Mr. Edgeworth, the Rector, would be only too pleased," Mr. Wilson said. "He's getting old, and he doesn't feel up to taking it himself. Mrs. Gore used to hold the class at the Rectory; there's a room there which is only used for parish meetings, and it has a piano in it and plenty of chairs."

"I'll ask him after Church tomorrow," Andrew's mother decided. "And meanwhile, Joanna, we'll be counting on you to bring some of the others along."

Chapter 5

HEATHER

JOANNA had been so happy at having made a friend, and so thrilled with the tracking and with Andrew's little farm, that she had actually forgotten about herself and her lameness. But at school on Monday morning, the old shyness and selfconsciousness returned, and she wondered how she could ever have imagined being able to talk to her schoolfellows about the new Sunday School.

During "break", all the others went about in pairs or formed little groups, and she found herself odd-man-out, as usual. It was not that any of them meant to be unkind or thoughtless. Some of the girls had tried to make friends with Joanna, but had given up after a time, as she seemed to prefer being by herself. Some of the more scatter-brained children were hardly aware of her lameness, which was not nearly so apparent as she imagined. To them, she seemed to be a sulky, unfriendly sort of person, and they soon forgot all about her.

There were plenty of other things to occupy their minds. There could be no organized games, now, as the school playing-field was covered with snow. But several snowmen were being made by different groups; there were snowball fights; and some had brought their sledges to school and were pulling each other about in them. The bigger boys had built a snow fort, and were defending it against a party of invaders, both sides being armed with snowballs. Joanna watched all these activities from a distance. It was easy enough, she thought moodily, for Andrew to talk of "roping in" people for his mother's class. No doubt he was popular at his school, and any suggestion he made would be received with enthusiasm.

"They should have asked someone like Heather to bring them," she thought. "The others will always listen to her; whatever she did, they would want to do it too!" She watched Heather Mitchell scoop up an armful of snow, and slap it on to the shoulders of the snowman she was helping to build. As usual, she was the centre and leader of the gayest group on the playing-field, and theirs was the tallest and most ambitious of the snowmen.

It was always a pleasure to watch Heather; all of her movements were so full of the joy of living, she seemed always to be dancing. Now she threw back her dark curly head and laughed for sheer happiness; stood on tiptoe to reach the top of the snowman, then swiftly stooped and swung up the smallest of her helpers, holding him while he modelled the snowman's face. Joanna turned away. One half of her longed to go on watching, the other felt half-resentful of Heather who was so different from herself.

Wandering towards the hedge that bounded

that side of the field, Joanna's attention was caught
by some marks in the snow. None of the children
had been over here, and the snow was still clean
and untrodden . . . untrodden, that is, by human
feet. Before she had known Andrew, she would
have said that there was nothing to be seen here at
all. But now she noticed the tracks of a rabbit—
of two rabbits—who had emerged from the hedge,
chased each other in circles and figures of eight, then
taken cover again. There were birds' prints, too;
tiny hopping birds which left their tracks in pairs,
and a larger bird which had walked . . . not sweeping its tail, so it could not have been a pheasant.
She wished she knew what bird it was—also that
she had brought her sketch-book so that she could
have made a drawing of the tracks.

A great black crow had just alighted on a deserted
part of the field and was walking about, vainly
searching for something to eat. Very slowly,
Joanna made her way towards him; but cautiously
though she moved, he saw her or heard her,
flapped his wings and soared into the air. But he
could not take his footprints with him. There were
his tracks, freshly made in the crisp snow, and
Joanna was nearly sure they were the same as the
prints by the hedge. Nearly certain—but not quite;
not yet being as experienced as Andrew, one large
bird's print looked, to her, very like another. If
only she could see them side by side . . . or if she
could have made a sketch . . . and suddenly she
knew what she must do. Stooping down, she
inserted her fingers very gingerly beneath one of

the prints, lifting the whole wedge of snow intact without disturbing the surface. Slowly, she straightened up and turned towards the hedge. . . .

"What *are* you doing?" She was so startled by hearing a voice close behind her, especially at recognizing the voice as Heather's, that she dropped the wedge of snow.

"Oh dear! Now it's all spoilt! Never mind; I can get another," she said, forgetting her shyness as she bent down to collect another specimen.

"But what *is* it? What are you trying to do?" Heather persisted, peering over Joanna's shoulder.

"I want to see if those tracks over by the hedge were made by a crow. I think they're the same as these . . . but I'm not sure, till I see them close together."

"How can you be certain that *these* are a crow's footmarks?" demanded Heather, bending over the trail.

"I know about these because I've just seen the crow walking here," explained Joanna. "Now— if I can carry this without spoiling the print, I'll be able to compare them."

"Shall I bring one too? Then if one gets spoilt, we'll have the other," suggested Heather.

Joanna nodded, secretly thrilled at Heather's eagerness to join in. Both prints were still intact by the time they reached the trail by the hedge, and Heather was as excited as Joanna on discovering that the original tracks had obviously been made by the same bird.

"And I think all these tiny marks must have been

chaffinches," Joanna said. "A whole flock of them
perched on the hedge, when I was here just now.
And this might be a thrush . . . no, a blackbird,
because it was running instead of hopping." She
pointed out the difference, then showed Heather
the rabbits' tracks; and a few minutes later, Heather
herself discovered some minute footprints which
they agreed could only be those of a field-mouse.

"Do you know, I've never properly noticed these
marks before!" exclaimed Heather. Already she
was completely absorbed; and this concentration
on the occupation of the moment was characteristic
of her. There was a look of wonder in her eyes—
the dark-blue eyes which were such a surprise in
her brown face. Other people became tanned only
during the summer months; but Heather kept her
glowing gipsy-colouring all the year round.

"I must have seen those tracks heaps of times,"
she went on. "But I'm such a mutt, I never knew
one could find out which creatures made which!"

"*I* never noticed them either, till last Saturday,"
Joanna confessed. "A boy called Andrew showed
me, and taught me about them. He has a little farm
of his own, and . . ." She had been on the verge of
telling Heather about Mrs. Fielding's plan for
starting a Sunday School; but before she could
begin, they were joined by Sally and Maureen who
had both come to see what Heather was doing.
Joanna suppressed a sigh. She might have known
that she would not get Heather to herself for long!
But her disappointment faded when she was asked
to explain about the tracks all over again, for the

benefit of the newcomers. Heather began trying to tell them; but she soon had to appeal to Joanna.

"Ask *her*! She knows all about them. She's just been showing me," she told the other girls. The bell rang while they were still hunting for fresh prints and trying to follow the various trails.

"Isn't it exciting? Like reading a marvellous book," Heather exclaimed as the four walked towards the school, the other girls suiting their pace to Joanna's. "If it hadn't been for Joanna, we'd all have gone on footling about and rushing around, knowing nothing about it! When can you show us some more, Jo?"

"There are lots of different prints down by the stream," Joanna told her. "But that's a bit far to go after school, perhaps."

"I've got to get home quickly, too," Heather remembered. "Rory, my puppy, will be waiting for me to take him for a run. He's the sweetest thing in the world! Have you seen him?"

"Well—only in the distance . . ." Joanna began; and then Heather said: "If you'll walk home with me, I'll show him to you. And we'll keep a look-out for tracks on the way."

Heather had asked her to walk home with her. She and Heather would be walking home together! This thought came between Joanna and her lessons during the afternoon classes. She had sometimes imagined such a thing happening, but had not dared hope for it, because she had been so sure that it would never come to pass. In spite of the hated surgical-boot with its thickened sole, she felt as if she were walking on air as she put away her books and pencils and fetched her brown coat and blue scarf and gloves from the cloakroom.

"Where's Joanna?" she heard Heather's voice asking. "Oh, *there* you are! Are you ready? Let's go, then."

If she had thought that there were to be just the two of them together, she was soon disappointed. Three other girls and two younger boys insisted on coming as far as Heather's house to see the new puppy. Heather walked beside Joanna, however, and didn't seem to find it strange to be plodding along at a steady pace, instead of skipping and dancing along the road in her usual manner—as if her body was made entirely of springs.

"Do find some more tracks, Jo! Can you see any?" she kept asking, as if Joanna were a magician and able to conjure them out of the air. The school stood at a short distance outside Hedley Green; but the road into the village was a fairly busy one, and there were few signs of wild life. The two girls and their companions amused themselves by comparing the different human footprints and guessing who they belonged to.

"This must have been a man . . . Mr. Hancock, perhaps. Look—it was a simply enormous foot!" cried one of the little boys. "I can get both my feet into one of his prints!"

"This one was wearing Wellington boots. I can see the pattern of the rubber," one of the girls exclaimed. Joanna found herself telling Heather, quite naturally, of how Andrew had tracked her on Saturday by the unusual print made by her big boot.

"Is your boot awfully heavy and tiring to walk with?" Heather asked, her dark-blue eyes full of sympathy. And Joanna admitted that yes, she did get tired fairly easily, though quite often she forgot all about it. Then they were in the village street and turned down a narrow by-road to reach Heather's home, which was one of a small row of cottages of the old-fashioned type.

"I always think these houses are so pretty; like something in a picture," Joanna said.

"Yes, they do look sweet, don't they?" Heather agreed. "Though I bet your house is heaps more comfortable—and modernized and all that. Still, this is all Dad can afford, at present. He teaches painting, you know, at a school in Northminster. But he's doing the work he likes best, and that's the main thing!"

The puppy was waiting for Heather in the tiny plot of garden in front of the cottage, his moist black nose pushed through the bars of the gate. He went nearly crazy with joy at the sight of his young mistress, and she seemed just as happy to see him. He was about six months old, brown, with a white chest and a dusky face.

"He's really rather a mixture—a mongrel," Heather confessed, when one of the girls asked what kind of dog he was. "But he's so clever and brave and affectionate, I wouldn't change him for the most valuable pedigree dog in the world. Would I,

Rory, my pet?" And Rory barked and rolled over and over in the snow, and careered round the garden, as if to show that he, too, was perfectly contented with his lot. They all wanted to play with Rory, and pet him; and the noise soon brought Mrs. Mitchell to the door to see what was going on. Heather's two little brothers were with her; she carried Nicky, the youngest, and held four-year-old Simon by the hand to prevent him from darting out into the snow after the puppy.

Heather gave her mother a hug, and immediately took charge of her brothers. Joanna noticed that mother and daughter were very much alike, though Mrs. Mitchell was smaller in build, and looked as if she worked too hard. Heather's manner towards her was gentle and protective, almost as if she were the mother and Mrs. Mitchell her child.

Joanna was so interested by this that she forgot the puppy for a moment. Seeing her eyes fixed on them, Heather called her to come indoors and be introduced, and let her hold Nicky, which she was secretly longing to do.

"I can see that you're used to babies, by the way you hold him," Mrs. Mitchell said. "Have you a little brother or sister of your own, dear?"

"No, I'm the only one." Joanna turned rather pink. "But I'd love to have a baby brother—exactly like Nicky."

"I'm afraid we can't spare Nick!" laughed Heather. "But you must come to tea one day, mustn't she, Mother? And you can help me give Nick his bath, and put him to bed."

"Yes, come any day you like," agreed Mrs. Mitchell. "Nicky seems to have taken to you; he's a bit shy with strangers, as a rule."

Joanna suddenly remembered how shy and awkward she usually was herself, and realized how queer it was that she should be standing in the Mitchells' kitchen, visiting their house for the first time, yet feeling completely happy and at home. It seemed quite natural to begin telling Heather and her mother about Andrew and Mrs. Fielding, and the plan for starting a Sunday School. Somehow Heather seemed more approachable here, with her family, than at school, where she was always surrounded by a crowd of other boys and girls. "I think I'd rather like to go to Sunday School," she said now. "Mother reads the Bible with me every evening; but it would be nice to have a special class for studying it."

"Especially as you keep asking questions which I'm not able to answer!" smiled Mrs. Mitchell. "Who else will be joining the class, Joanna, besides yourself and Andrew?" Joanna had to admit that nobody else knew of the class, as yet. "Mrs. Fielding asked me to let them know, at school," she added. "But I—I didn't know how to begin."

"We'll talk to them about it tomorrow," Heather said promptly. "I'm sure there are lots of people who'll want to join, when we tell them about it."

Joanna nodded agreement, without saying what was in her mind: that there would be no lack of recruits for the class once it was known that Heather intended to join it.

Chapter 6

NEW PLANS

"WHATEVER made you so late?" Mrs. Wilson asked, when Joanna reached home. "Andrew Fielding has been here; he was on his way from school. He got off the bus when it stopped in the village, and walked the rest of the way home. He looked in here to see you . . . but he couldn't stop long, as his mother would have been wondering where he was."

"I wish I hadn't missed him," exclaimed Joanna. "I went home with Heather Mitchell, and saw her puppy and her little brothers. But I'd have left sooner, if I'd known Andrew was here."

Her mother glanced at her in surprise. Joanna usually arrived back silent and depressed after her day at school, having walked home alone. She had seemed to want to avoid the other children, and certainly never made friends with any of them. It really looked as if she might be going to come out of her shell at last.

"Andrew was asking if you could go home with him, some days, and help with his farm-work—as he calls it," Mrs. Wilson told Joanna. "He says he'd get off the bus and call for you, like he did today. Or, if you can get to the bus-stop in time, when you've finished school, you can get on the bus and

go along with him. He seemed so set on the idea
. . . but I didn't really know what to say——"

"Oh, Mummy, *could* I? Please! I would so love
it!" Although Joanna's thoughts had beeen full of
Heather's friendliness and of the visit to her home,
she had not forgotten Andrew's farm, nor the lovely
time she had spent at Stone House on Saturday.
The memory of it had been a warm, happy spot
at the back of her mind. Now she thought again of
the hens, the ducks, the geese and the trim bantams;
the happy importance of mixing the pigs' food to
exactly the right consistency; the excitement of
learning to milk the goats. If she could go there
every day, or even two or three times a week, she
would learn to be really useful. She wouldn't be just
doing it for fun; it would be real important work.

"Do let me go!" she begged.

"I'll have to ask Dad about it," her mother said.
"Now that the days are lengthening, I don't see
why you shouldn't go there sometimes. Andrew
says that his mother is willing to see you home, like
she did Saturday. But we'll hear what Dad has to
say."

Joanna's father was employed by the Electricity
Board, and went into Northminster every day on
his motor-bike. When he got home, he was surprised
to see the door flung open by Joanna, who had been
listening eagerly for the sound of his machine. He
was still more surprised to hear his quiet, solemn
little daughter talking so fast and so excitedly that
it was some time before he was able to follow what
she was saying. When she finished by asking:

"So you will say yes, won't you, Dad? I've always wanted to work on a farm"—he turned to his wife and asked, "What was that all about?"

While he was having his tea, Mrs. Wilson told him of Andrew's request; and, to Joanna's disappointment, he replied that he wanted a little time to think it over.

"We'll let you know in the morning," he told her. "You go off to bed, now, like a good girl, and we'll talk about it again tomorrow."

What he really wanted was to discuss the matter with his wife when Joanna was not with them. There had been a time when they had treated their child as if she had been a fragile piece of china; keeping her with them as much as possible, always afraid that she might get hurt or over-tired if she played with other children. Then Doctor Fairfax explained to them that the best medicine for Joanna would be to treat her as if there were nothing wrong with her at all.

"She's perfectly strong and healthy, now," he pointed out. "Or she would be, if you didn't keep her wrapped in cotton-wool, so to speak! Of course her lameness will be a handicap where some games are concerned; otherwise, she should lead a perfectly normal life, and be with kids of her own age as much as possible."

Joanna's parents quite understood the wisdom of this advice; but her own shyness and self-consciousness had made it very difficult for them to put it into practice. Andrew's suggestion that she should help him with his farm seemed like an answer to their prayers; and they had only to make sure that both felt the same way about it, before deciding to let her try the plan—two or three times a week, to start with.

"We could say Tuesdays and Thursdays, weather permitting," Mrs. Wilson said. "And she can go there for longer on Saturdays, if she likes, and if he wants her."

Mr. Wilson made one condition, and that was that he could not accept Mrs. Fielding's offer to see Joanna home. His motor-bike had a side-car attached; and he himself would collect Joanna when he came home from work.

Joanna didn't make the mistake of expecting that, from now on, she and Heather would be inseparable. For one thing, Heather was a year older than herself; for another, she was far too warmhearted and friendly by nature to single out one particular person, shutting out all the rest. Some of the other girls went about in pairs, giggling and pretending to have important secrets, and making everybody else feel left out in the cold. But Heather's friendliness included everyone with whom she came in contact; and Joanna was quite content to be one of the many.

Heather beckoned to her in break, however, and asked her for some details about the proposed Sunday School. She had been talking about it to three other girls—Daphne, Pat, and Maureen—and they all wanted to join it. But Daphne's parents always took her to see her granny on Sundays, and she would not be able to attend the class if it took place too late in the afternoon.

"I'll ask Mrs. Fielding," Joanna promised. "I'll be going to Stone House after school today."

This led to her telling them about Andrew's farm; and Heather asked so many questions and seemed so interested in it, that Joanna secretly made up her mind to ask Andrew if he could do with another assistant on Saturdays. By the time school broke up, nearly everyone had heard about the Sunday School plan; and so many said they wanted to come, that Joanna began to wonder whether the room at the Rectory would hold them all.

Chapter 7

TRACKING IN THE SNOW

MRS. FIELDING was delighted to hear that Joanna had collected so many recruits for the class.

"Don't worry about the numbers, though," she said. "I daresay they won't all turn up, when it comes to the point; and even if they do, we'll manage somehow."

She had come into the paddock to tell Joanna that Mr. Wilson had arrived to fetch her home; and they were walking back to the house, leaving Andrew to finish the remaining chores.

"I've just been telling Andrew, I think a lot of them are only coming because of Heather," Joanna said. "I believe only a few of them are really keen on Sunday School; the rest just want to do what Heather does."

"Never mind. It'll all sort itself out," Mrs. Fielding said cheerfully. "Meanwhile, you can be finding out what time of day suits the greatest number of people, and let me know when you come here on Thursday."

It was on Thursday that Joanna began to feel that she was really being of use to Andrew. He was able to leave the feeding of the poultry entirely to her, and she only needed a little help in herding

43

them into their sleeping quarters. Meanwhile he had fed the pigs and milked one of the goats; and she was able to milk Mandy, the quiet one, all by herself, as they were well ahead of time. He gladly fell in with the suggestion that Heather should be asked to join them on Saturday. "And if there are any others you'd like to bring, I'm sure Mum won't mind having a few extra for tea," he added. "We could organize a tracking game, if the snow hasn't thawed by then."

They were eagerly discussing this when they heard Mr. Wilson's motor-bike approaching—earlier than they had expected him.

"Oh, Dad! Why did you come so soon?" she exclaimed, when Mrs. Fielding brought him out to the paddock to find her.

"That's a nice sort of welcome to get, at the end of a hard day's work!" he complained, pretending to be hurt.

"Are you in a hurry, sir? Or would you like to see the farm?" asked Andrew.

"That's partly why I came so early," Joanna's father admitted. "That is, if you can do with us for a few minutes longer?" he added, turning to Mrs. Fielding.

"We'd like you to stay as long as you can," she replied, putting her arm round Joanna.

So Mr. Wilson was taken on a special conducted tour of Andrew's smallholding, and was very much impressed by all he saw.

"Joanna tells me you are keen on birds, and wild life in general," he said to Andrew, when they had returned to the house. "I saw something on my way here, which I think might interest you. It's getting too dark to see much now; but if you stand still and listen, you'll hear something that will surprise you."

"Andrew *can't* listen," Joanna reminded him.

"Sorry, old chap! You lip-read so well, I keep forgetting you can't hear," her father said, smiling at Andrew. "But I'll show Joanna the place, and she can take you there another day before it's too dark."

He stopped the motor-bike by a gate which led into a field close to Stone House, and told Joanna to get out of the side-car and listen. It was true that it was getting nearly dark; but from a wooded hollow in the middle of the field, Joanna could hear a curious sound . . . a regular din, rather like a crowd of quarrelsome children all squabbling together.

"What is it?" she whispered. "It's—they're *birds*, aren't they? But—there must be hundreds and hundreds of them!"

"Starlings—that's what they are," Mr. Wilson told her. "Thousands of them; come from over the sea—from Denmark, probably—searching for food. I've heard there's a regular plague of them in these parts; and at night, they'll settle in one place, like that little copse there, and go off scavenging again in the morning. Just you come and stand here one afternoon, when the light's beginning to fade, and you'll see them coming in, from all directions."

The plans for Saturday were mounting up at such a rate, Joanna doubted whether they would all fit into one day. To begin with, she had promised to spend part of the morning helping Andrew to clean out the poultry-houses, shift some of the runs, and give the pigs a fresh supply of straw. Mrs. Fielding had invited her to lunch; and afterwards, Heather, Sally and Maureen were coming to join them in a tracking game. Heather wanted to stay and help feed the animals and poultry after the game; and now Andrew was determined to get his jobs done in time to go and watch for the starlings which Joanna had told him about. The weather was grey and dull on Saturday morning, and Joanna was in a fever lest it should rain and spoil the tracking.

"I was so afraid the snow wouldn't last till today!" she told Andrew, who had walked along the road to meet her.

"We could have looked for tracks in the mud, even if the snow *had* gone," he retorted. "Though they're easier to see in the snow, of course."

"But we couldn't have played the tracking game without the snow, could we?" she asked.

"Yes, we could; by laying Scout signs. I think it's more fun that way, really; I'll show you, one day. But we must get on with our work, now, or we'll never be done before lunch."

It was Joanna's first experience of hard physical work, and she enjoyed every minute of it. Cleaning out the houses was rather a messy, smelly job; but there was all the greater satisfaction in knowing that the creatures were tidy and comfortable again, and in adding fresh barrowfuls to the valuable heap of manure in the corner of the vegetable-garden. All the water-troughs and bowls were given a special wash on Saturdays, so that the whole farm had a regular "spring-clean" once a week.

"We'll need a spring-cleaning ourselves, before we go in to lunch!" laughed Joanna, when at last they had finished. Andrew looked at his wrist-watch.

"It isn't lunch-time yet," he said. "I wish it was; I'm frightfully hungry."

"So am I! Starving!" agreed Joanna, wondering what her mother would say if she could hear her.

"Let's go and look for tracks in the field where you heard the starlings," Andrew suggested. "Bring your sketch-book, because I saw a hare there yesterday, when I went down to catch the bus."

They found the hare's trail, and Joanna sketched the prints, which were like a rabbit's, only larger and further apart. She wanted to draw every track she saw; but Andrew persuaded her to keep the collection only to those prints which they could identify, and leave out anything they were not sure about. They added the prints of several birds to the collection, including those made by the webbed feet of the many gulls which had flown inland from the coast; and the trail of a prowling cat was easy to identify.

Then they inspected the starlings' encampment, and saw how the twigs and shoots of the young trees were broken by the weight of the roosting birds.

When the Irish stew and boiled apple-pudding had been dispatched as if by magic, they did the washing-up between them while Mrs. Fielding went back to her typing. She was typing a book for a well-known author, one of many who sent her their manuscripts to prepare for publication. When they had finished their work, Andrew and Joanna went to stand at the gate, to wait for Heather and the other girls. Andrew was secretly wishing that he was not to be the only boy in the party, when three figures appeared round the bend. Not three girls, as he had expected, but two girls and a boy.

"Why it's—I think it's Peter, Maureen's brother," whispered Joanna. "He's about my age, I think; and Heather and Maureen are twelve. But—I wonder what's happened to Sally!"

"Poor Sally has a cold, and her mother made her stay indoors," Heather explained. When Joanna had told him their names, she reminded them to look straight at him when they talked, so that he could lip-read.

"Was it all right to bring Peter?" Maureen asked anxiously. "He begged and begged to come, but we said he couldn't because your mother was only expecting three."

"But when Sally dropped out, we thought perhaps you wouldn't mind," Heather finished for her.

"I'm awfully glad," Andrew said, looking at the sturdy Peter with great satisfaction. "What would you all like to do first?"

"Can I see the farm, please?" Peter said—so promptly that they all laughed. But as it was just

what Heather and Maureen wanted too, Andrew
and Joanna led the way round the house, through
the garden to the paddock. When all the creatures
had been inspected, Andrew suggested that they
should start their game. They were to have tea
early, as Maureen and Peter had promised not to be
late home; but Heather was in no particular hurry,
and it was arranged that she and Joanna would
help Andrew feed the animals after tea.

"I vote we draw lots for who lays the trail,"
Andrew said. "Look—these five bits of straw will
do; we'll shut out eyes and take one each. The two
with the longest straws can be hares, and the rest
hounds."

They shut their eyes and each pulled one of the
straws held by Andrew; and when they compared
them, it was agreed that Heather's and Joanna's
were easily the longest.

"It'll be scrummy, having Joanna as one of the
hares," remarked Peter, who was nothing if not
outspoken. "We'll easily sort out her track from the
others, because her boot is different."

Maureen slapped her brother; but Andrew
calmly agreed that it was just as well to have an
easy trail to follow, this first time. And Joanna
realized that Peter's thoughtless words had not
made her feel cross and miserable as they would
have done in the past.

"We'll give you a good five minutes start,"
Andrew said, remembering that Joanna could not
get along very fast. "I don't suppose we'll actually
catch up with you; so mind you notice the time

when you get back to the house, so we'll know how much longer we've been."

"I haven't been in this part before," Heather said, when the hounds had gone into the house. "I wonder which way we'd better go?"

"I know it fairly well," Joanna said shyly. She was unaccustomed to taking the lead, and it seemed odd to be giving advice to Heather, of all people. "Mummy and I come nearly as far as this, when we go blackberrying; and Andrew took me a walk round the fields this morning."

"Did you go up there?" asked Heather, pointing to a little hill beyond the starlings' field. She never remained very long in a state of indecision, and now felt that she could soon map out a course if they could get on to some high ground. "I mean—is there any private land in between, where we are not allowed to go?" she added, rather impatiently. "We must hurry up and start; they'll be after us directly."

"I don't think any of it's private," Joanna said. They had started walking towards the field beyond the paddock, and now she broke into a sort of uneven jog-trot which was the nearest she could get to running. "We went round by the lane this morning; but I think there's a short cut this way."

From the field next to the paddock, they squeezed through a wire fence into the starlings' field.

"Are you all right, going at this pace? I mean, you won't hurt yourself or anything, will you?" Heather asked anxiously, as they jogged through the snow.

"No, it won't do any harm," Joanna assured her. "Look—that's where we went this morning; you can see our tracks." Her eyes sparkled with mischief. "I was just wondering if we could play a sort of trick on them . . . to give us a bit more of a start, as I'm so slow. Your boots are nearly the same size as Andrew's——"

"And if we mix our footprints with the ones you and he made this morning, we'll get them nicely muddled!" finished Heather, laughing delightedly.

They followed the morning's trail until it led them to some trees beneath which the snow had thawed so that their feet left no prints. Here they broke away from the old trail and crawled through a hedge.

"With any luck, that should throw them off the scent for a few minutes," remarked Heather, as they scrambled up a slope towards the brow of the hill. "Look out! Let's get the other side of those gorse-bushes. They might easily see us, now we're on high ground."

The spirit of the chase had got into them. Joanna's heart was thumping—and not only from the effort of climbing the snowy slope. They breathed more easily when they had taken cover; but they didn't talk any more till they reached the group of stunted windswept oak-trees at the top. Then. . . . "Look! Oh—look!" panted Joanna. Far away below they could see Stone House and the paddock behind it; and in the field next to it, the figures of their three pursuers ran swiftly across the snow, squeezed through the wire fence, then checked when they came to the trail which the two hares had deliberately confused with the earlier one.

"That'll hold them up for a bit!" chuckled Heather. "How tiny they look from here!"

Her eyes swept the country below them, mapping out a route which would eventually lead them back to Stone House. "Come on!" She grasped Joanna's arm. "Down this side, and along that cart-track at the bottom."

"That cart-track leads to the big farm," gasped Joanna as she stumbled and slithered down the hillside. "If we go . . . through the farmyard . . . they won't find it so easy to . . . follow . . . our tracks."

"Good idea! The snow will be all trampled and churned up by the animals and tractors and things," Heather agreed. "Oh Jo! Isn't this exciting? Just like having a real adventure!"

Joanna, too, had found herself forgetting that it was only a game, and felt as if everything depended on their reaching Stone House without being caught. They could neither see nor hear the hounds, but guessed that they could not be far behind.

"Andrew will have seen through our trick quite soon," muttered Joanna. "He'll remember where we went this morning and he'll soon pick up the fresh trail."

It took longer than they had expected to reach the farm; but when they got there they found, as they had guessed, that it would be easy to throw the others off the scent for a while. Their own footprints were lost among hoof-marks and the tracks of many wheels; and they left the farmyard, not by the most obvious route, but through a gap in the hedge by the horsepond. Down another cart-track, over a bank, and across three more fields where their footprints stood out once more, clear and easy to follow. Then over a stile, which brought them into the lane which ran past Stone House . . . and they were home.

Chapter 8

TEA AT STONE HOUSE

"WE'VE had such a *gorgeous* time!" Heather exclaimed, as Mrs. Fielding opened the door for them. "Jo's a splendid hare; she had all the best ideas for throwing the hounds off the scent."

"I expect you both want to rest your legs," Mrs. Fielding said. "Take off your coats, and come and sit down in here till the others arrive."

Joanna had not realized how tired she was, till she sank down beside Heather on the sitting-room sofa. She had made a great effort to keep going, as she had been so afraid of being a drag on Heather, who was so active and athletic.

"I'm sure you must be Heather!" Mrs. Fielding said, smiling at the older girl. "Aren't you the kind person who has been getting the Sunday School class together for me?"

"Well, it's been Jo's doing, really——" Heather began, but Joanna interrupted her.

"No, it was Heather who did all the talking to people," she said. "I got in a panic about it! And anyway, no one would have wanted to join if *I'd* asked them." She spoke in the bitter discouraged tone to which her parents were only too well accustomed; but Mrs. Fielding had never heard her speak like that before, and both she and Heather looked at Joanna in surprise.

"Why—you silly old Jo, you asked *me*—and *I* wanted to join!" protested Heather. "What difference could it possibly make, whether you tackled them or I did?"

Joanna wanted to say that there was all the difference in the world, but somehow she couldn't put it into words. She appealed to Mrs. Fielding. "*You* see what I mean, don't you?" she asked.

"I can understand your feeling as you do," Mrs. Fielding said thoughtfully. "But I'm not sure that I agree with you. I believe that God means to use both you *and* Heather as His 'messengers' . . . though in different ways, perhaps. It's possible that *you* may be used even more than she is, just because you have special difficulties to overcome."

"That's what I was thinking!" Heather said eagerly. "Jo is so brave about her lameness, and though she can't run and jump and play netball, she's marvellous at drawing; and she tracks birds and animals, and finds all sorts of interesting things to do. People would pay far more attention to her, than to an ordinary person like me."

Mrs. Fielding reached for a Bible which lay on a table near her chair, and turned the pages till she came to St. Paul's Epistle to the Corinthians.

"This is a letter, written by one of the greatest of our Lord's messengers," she said. "St. Paul, too, had a physical difficulty to overcome; he said of himself: '. . . his bodily presence is weak'. He described it as 'a thorn in the flesh', and went on to say: 'For this thing I besought the Lord thrice, that it might depart from me. And He said unto me: *My Grace is sufficient for thee: for My strength is made perfect in weakness.* Most gladly, therefore, will I rather glory in my infirmities, that the power of Christ may rest upon me. Therefore I take pleasure in my infirmities. . . .' I expect, at first, Paul felt just like you do, Joanna. He prayed and prayed that our Lord would heal him—as He had healed so many others. But in time he came to glory in his infirmities, as something to be *used* in Christ's service."

Joanna said nothing; but her shining eyes showed that she had understood. And just then, the sound of cheerful breathless voices announced the arrival of the hounds.

"That was a fine trick you played on us, Jo!" exclaimed Andrew. "Especially as I'd clean forgotten that we went that way this morning. We followed the wrong trail for simply ages——"

"And we lost the trail altogether in the farm-yard," added Peter. "Only that Andrew has eyes like a hawk, we'd have been there still!"

They all sat down to tea chattering and laughing, and going over the details of the chase. And it was then that Joanna noticed how often Andrew got left out of the conversation. Having frequently felt out of things herself, she was more sensitive than the others; and she saw how they sometimes turned away from him when they were talking, so that he couldn't lip-read. When this happened he waited patiently till he was able to join in again. But it made him seem very lonely, and Joanna's heart ached for him. She thought over all the fun she had had during the past week; the fresh interests and the new friendships, and the difference they had made in her life. And she remembered that it had all started with that chance meeting with Andrew. She owed it all to this boy who was so brave and cheerful about his deafness—his infirmity.

"And it's his deafness that has made him so noticing and understanding," she thought. "If he hadn't been like that, I could never have made friends with him; and none of these lovely things would have happened!"

Maureen said that she and Peter ought to be thinking about getting home. "Can't we stay and feed the pigs?" asked Peter, who had been talking about the farm with Andrew.

"Mum said we were to be back before dark," his sister reminded him. "And I know what'll happen if you once start helping Andrew!"

"We'll come with you as far as the main road," Andrew said. "There'll be plenty of time to do the feeding and milking afterwards, if Heather and Jo are both going to help."

The light was beginning to fade, however, by the time they reached the end of the lane and had waved good-bye to Maureen and Peter. And then, as Andrew and his two helpers were hurrying back to the house, he suddenly remembered what Joanna had told him about the starlings.

"Let's stop for a minute for two," he said, when they reached the gate which led into the field.

"Oh!" cried both the girls at once. "What is it?

Whatever is happening?" For it had suddenly become much darker, as if a great black cloud had swept across the sky; and there was a rustling whirring sound overhead.

"It's the starlings!" gasped Andrew. "Look! Hundreds and hundreds of them."

It was light once more; and now the girls looked up and saw the huge flock of birds receding in the distance; wheeling like well-drilled soldiers, then circling round and round in ever-smaller circles, till they dropped—by twenties, thirties, fifties, into the wooded hollow. They could hear the squabbling, chattering noise of the birds as they jostled each other for a foothold in the branches; then, again, there was the sound as of a rushing, tearing wind, and another flock—like a winged army—swept overhead, shutting out the light.

"There's another lot coming—look! Right away over there!" Andrew pointed to the north; then glancing round, saw yet another flock approaching from the opposite direction. The three children watched in silence, fascinated by the strange sight. From north, north-east and east; from the south, south-west and west; from every point of the compass came the hordes and regiments of starlings. Each flock circled round and round in exactly the same way, obeying some law known only to themselves. And all finally descended into the hollow, to join their noisy, chattering companions.

The girls would have been ready to stay there, watching and listening, until it was dark; but Andrew dragged them away, sternly reminding them that there was work to be done before night-fall.

As it was so late, he milked both the goats himself, leaving Joanna to deal with the poultry with Heather's assistance. Even so, they had barely finished by the time Mr. Wilson arrived with the motor-bike to fetch the two girls. There was a scramble then to get finished. They had to go into the house to say good-bye to Mrs. Fielding and collect Joanna's sketch-book; and Andrew gave each of the girls a bantam's egg for tomorrow's breakfast. Then he and his mother came to the gate to see the girls squeeze into the side-car.

"Don't forget—Sunday School at two o'clock, at the Rectory," Mrs. Fielding reminded them.

"It looks as if there'll be about thirty of us! Can you manage all that crowd?" Heather asked anxiously.

"The more the merrier! But don't be dis-appointed if they don't all turn up," Mrs. Fielding warned her, as Mr. Wilson started the engine.

Chapter 9

THE RESCUE OF RORY

LIKE so many lively people, Heather was subject to abrupt changes of mood. She always expected to enjoy herself and usually did so, infecting all around her with her sparkling high spirits. But every now and then she would become dull and listless, her spirits would flag, and she would lose interest in what she was doing.

These dull moods had a depressing effect on her companions, so it was fortunate that they did not happen very often, and never lasted for long. She had a bad attack of "the doldrums", however, on that Sunday which was to see the start of the new Sunday School. As she had told Mrs. Fielding, about thirty boys and girls had said they wanted to join it; and she was bitterly disappointed to find, when the day came, that more than half of them had dropped out. Some had colds, some were being taken by their parents to visit a granny or other relatives; while some had simply lost interest in the idea. Besides herself, Joanna and Andrew, only eight others turned up, making eleven in all; and as their ages varied between twelve and five, it was a difficult class to organize.

Mrs. Fielding had expected something of the sort, and had already planned to put one of the older girls, probably Heather herself, in charge of the little ones for part of the time; they were to colour Bible pictures or texts while she gave more advanced teaching to the others. But Heather was gloomy and depressed, and showed no interest in this or any other plan. Her mood had infected the rest of the class, and not one of them seemed prepared to be helpful.

Mrs. Fielding decided to take no notice of the yawning and fidgeting; and having started them off with a lively hymn, she made them all sit down while she asked them why they had come to Sunday School.

Everyone was surprised by the question, and there was a pause before someone replied: "To learn about God." After this, Mrs. Fielding kept them all on the alert by quickly firing off questions— first at one, then at another:

"Why do we want to learn about Him? How can we get to know Him? How can we learn how to please Him?" Then she led them all in a simple prayer, after which she told those who had Bibles to turn to the fourteenth chapter of St. John's Gospel, and find the words: "I am the way". Teaching them by question and answer, so that their attention never had time to wander, she explained that it was only through Jesus Christ that they could get to know God; and she told them of the calling of the first disciples, to whom Christ had said: "Follow Me".

Then she asked Andrew to describe the tracking game they had played the day before, to show how much patience and perseverance is needed to follow the right way.

"What did you do when you lost the trail for a time?" she asked him. "Did you wander off aimlessly, choosing a way of your own? Or did you give up and go home?"

"Of course we didn't!" laughed Andrew. "We kept close to where we had last seen the signs; and we kept on going back to that place, till we'd picked up the trail again. Guessing, and taking short-cuts is usually a waste of time, when you're tracking someone."

By this time, every member of the class was wide awake and interested. When Joanna was asked to read aloud the verses from Psalms 25 and 31:

"Show me thy ways, O Lord, and teach me thy paths. Lead me forth in thy truth and learn me. . . . Be thou also my guide, and lead me for thy name's sake"
they listened attentively.

"I want you to learn these words by heart," Mrs. Fielding said, when she had made them repeat the verses several times. "Perhaps the older ones would help the little ones—so that you can all say them to me next Sunday. And at the next class, we will learn *how* our Lord shows us the Way. You see, sometimes He only shows us one step at a time. And, like in the tracking game, we shall only get lost if we try to run on ahead of what He has shown us, or take short-cuts, or go off on our own."

When the class broke up, Heather and Joanna stayed behind to help Andrew and his mother tidy the room.

"I'm sorry I was such a wet-blanket to start with," Heather said, as they left the Rectory. "I felt a bit fed up with all those others who had promised to come. And I was worried about Rory, too. Someone left the gate open, and I can't think where he's got to."

"Oh Heather—I *am* sorry. No wonder you were feeling anxious," Mrs. Fielding exclaimed.

"Has he ever got out before?" Andrew wanted to know.

"Yes—but he never went very far. I'm so afraid he may have got on to the main road."

Heather sounded as if she was very near tears; but she was grateful when Joanna and Andrew said they would go home with her and help look for the puppy.

"I hope you'll find him waiting for you, when you get home," Mrs. Fielding said, as they left her.

But there was no excited little dog poking his nose through the bars of the gate; and Heather's parents said that there had been no news of him, though they had been making inquiries among all the neighbours.

At any other time, Joanna would have been thrilled at meeting Mr. Mitchell, because he was a real artist. But now she could think of nothing but poor little Rory. Then Andrew, who had wandered off by himself, came back to report that he had found the puppy's tracks in the snow. "He didn't go towards the main road at all—but in the opposite direction," he said.

"*Andrew!* How clever of you! Why ever didn't I

think of that?" exclaimed Heather, as she and Joanna followed him. The snow near the houses had been trodden down hard, and had even disappeared altogether in some places. But Andrew's practised eyes had found prints of the little pads here and there, and had finally picked up a clearly marked trail out in the open country.

Rory had squeezed through the hedge to get into a field on the other side; and the three trackers had to go on down the by-road to find an opening, then walk back along the hedge to rejoin the trail. Finding himself in a large empty field, Rory had spent a little while careering round in circles to work off his high spirits. Then something at the other side of the field must have attracted his attention, for he had trotted off in a straight line towards the opposite hedge. Here the snow had drifted and was quite deep; the puppy had clearly got into difficulties, as there were signs that he had struggled and floundered about in the drift.

"Poor little Rory! You don't think he could be under this snow, do you?" whispered Joanna.

Heather turned pale; but now Andrew called that he could see the trail in the field beyond.

"Brave little chap! He got through somehow, and he's been after a rabbit," he shouted.

The girls scrambled through and joined Andrew, who pointed to a line of rabbit's tracks, with which the puppy's prints had mingled. Rory had followed the rabbit as far as a clump of alder-bushes. Here the rabbit had taken refuge in a hole, and the puppy had made a gallant effort to dig it out. The snow had thawed under the alders, and a little heap of freshly-dug earth proved how hard Rory had worked.

"You can see where he has gnawed through the roots of the trees," Andrew showed them.

"Do you think . . . could he possibly be down there, still?" Heather asked shakily. "He's so small —he might easily wriggle down a rabbit-hole and get stuck."

Andrew lay flat on the ground and thrust his arm down the hole. "He couldn't have got down there," he announced, getting up and brushing the earth from his arm. "We must cast around, like real hounds do, until we find the scent again."

"Casting" consisted of searching the ground in ever-increasing circles round the last place where they had seen a print. All three were remembering what Mrs. Fielding had said about the Christian life; how we are sometimes led only a little way at a time, and must follow faithfully, step by step, keeping close to our Guide.

It was Joanna who first caught sight of the fresh line of tracks, among the many prints of birds and animals. Rory had evidently started to make his way home; but had changed his mind and turned aside, perhaps to go after a bird.

"See how fast he was moving. He must have been chasing something," Andrew said, pointing to the different formation of the tracks which led them to an overgrown hedge on a high bank. They had to go some distance along the hedge before they could find a way through; but though they walked up and down on the other side, there was no sign of Rory's footprints.

"Listen!" Heather said suddenly, clutching Andrew's arm and forgetting that he could hear nothing. "Wait! Yes—there it is again."

Joanna heard it this time . . . a faint but unmistakable yelp, followed by a whine, as of a little dog in distress. Joanna explained to Andrew, then they both followed Heather who had set off at a run in the direction from which the sound had come. When they caught up with her, she was kneeling in the snow with her arms round the bedraggled and whimpering puppy.

"His leg's caught in something; it feels like a piece of wire," she gasped. "He must have struggled and struggled . . . I can't get at it, when he won't keep still."

In a moment Andrew was on his knees beside her. "Try and hold him still," he said. "Yes—I thought so! It's a snare." He drew a forked stick out of the ground, to which a wire noose had been attached with string. Rory had caught his paw in the noose, and his struggles had only pulled it tighter, so that the wire was now imbedded in his fur. Andrew worked gently at the wire to loosen it, and finally released the puppy, who went nearly crazy with joy. Heather was just as bad; she hugged her dog and hugged Andrew—who hardly noticed, being intent on examining the snare.

"These are illegal now, you know," he said. "It must have been set by a poacher to catch a rabbit, or even a pheasant. We ought to take it to the police,

I think. Suppose the poor little dog had had this round his neck!"

The girls were so busy petting Rory, who licked his bruised paw, whining to them for sympathy, then forgot it in his joy at being released—that they didn't hear heavy footsteps crunching through the snow.

"What are you doing with that?" asked a gruff voice; and looking round, they saw a boy of about eighteen, who stood scowling at them with his hands in his pockets. There was an expression on his face which made Heather pick Rory up and hold him safely in her arms. Andrew had heard nothing; but on catching sight of the stranger, he faced him calmly and fearlessly.

"Is this yours?" he asked, holding out the snare. The youth snatched it out of his hands, snarling: "You give that here, and stop meddling with what don't concern you." He thrust the snare into one of the deep pockets of his dirty jacket; then he glared at the children as if he would have liked to say more.

"My puppy got caught in that horrid thing . . . and he might have died of cold and hunger if we hadn't found him," Heather blurted out indignantly. The boy muttered something about "a good riddance"; then he turned and tramped away towards a gate and vaulted over it. The children stood watching until he was out of sight.

"We ought to report him to the police. Who is he, do you know?" asked Andrew. The girls shook their heads.

"I've never seen him before," Heather said.

"Shall we follow him, and try to find out where he lives?"

"He may not go straight home," Andrew pointed out. "If he has set other snares, he'll be doing a round of them to see if he's caught anything."

His eyes were on the ground; and now he pulled a pencil from his pocket and fumbled about till he found a scrap of paper.

"Could you make a sketch of his footprints, Jo?" he asked. "It mightn't be a bad plan to have a record of them . . . in case there's any more trouble."

Joanna blushed with pleasure at being called on to do this important piece of detective-work; and she carefully drew the print made by the hobnailed boot while the others watched admiringly.

"You see where the left sole is worn at the side?" Andrew said, examining the tracks. "And there's an unevenness where some of the nails are missing. Well done, Jo! We may find this useful, one day."

Heather was the least interested of the three in following up the setter of illegal snares. Her one thought now was to get her precious Rory safe home, and to reassure her parents.

"Couldn't you come in for a few minutes?" she asked Joanna, when they got back to the village. Andrew was going straight to Stone House to see to his animals, but Joanna was in no hurry, and she was glad to be present at Rory's homecoming. She and Heather knelt on each side of him while he lapped up the hot dinner which Mrs. Mitchell had prepared for him. Heather had eyes for nothing but her dog; but Joanna kept glancing towards the window where Mr. Mitchell sat at a table, looking through a pile of black-and-white drawings.

"Like to come and see?" he offered, smiling at her eager face. He explained then that he had been commissioned to do the illustrations for a children's book. The publishers had sent him the manuscript, saying how many illustrations were needed; and the artist had to choose which scenes in the story could best be made into pictures.

"You'd better ask Jo to do some of them for you," remarked Heather, who had joined them, holding Rory in her arms. "She draws and paints beautifully —far better than anyone else in the school."

Mr. Mitchell was interested at once; and Joanna didn't know whether she was more pleased or embarrassed when he asked her to bring some of her drawings to show him.

"Though I can't let you cut me out in this particular job!" he added with a twinkle. "These illustrations are to earn a little extra money . . . and I happen to need it for something very important!"

Heather put Rory down, and threw her arms round her father's neck. "Isn't he a darling?" she exclaimed to Joanna. "Working every evening when he gets back from school . . . and all so that he can buy me a bicycle!"

Chapter 10

TRACKING WITH SIGNS

HEATHER'S bicycle arrived when the last of the snow had been washed away by a night of heavy rain. It had been gradually thawing for several days; there was no more tobogganning, and even Andrew had to admit that tracking games were over for the present, unless played in the Scouts' way, making their own signs. He had promised to teach these to Joanna, Heather, and some of the others; but before Saturday came, Heather had got her new bicycle. For the time being, she could think of nothing else, and Joanna had one of her sharpest stabs of envy and discontent as she watched Heather and several of her friends taking turns to ride it up and down the road outside the Mitchells' house. They had all come to see the bicycle, and with her usual generosity Heather was letting everyone have a ride . . . everyone except Joanna, who could only look on.

She heard the Northminster bus stop in the main street, and wished she could have boarded it and gone on with Andrew to Stone House. But it was not one of her days for going to the farm; and though he and his mother had urged her to come whenever she liked, she only had her own parents' permission to go there on Tuesdays, Thursdays, and Saturdays.

She had just made up her mind to go home, and had turned away from the excited group of would-be cyclists, when she saw the tall, thin figure of Mr. Mitchell striding towards her.

"Hello! You're the very person I want!" he exclaimed. "I've just got off the bus, and I nearly went straight to your home to look for you. But I thought you might be with Heather, so I came here first."

Then he told her that he had met her father in Northminster, and had had a talk with him about Joanna's drawings—which she had, rather unwillingly, allowed Heather to take home one evening.

"Your drawings show a good deal of promise, perhaps even talent," he said. "Have you ever thought of taking it up seriously, later on?"

She went very red and stared at the muddy road. "It's what I like doing best," she muttered. "But— I don't know—I didn't think I'd ever be good enough."

"How would you like to come and work with me after school, once a week?" he asked. "I hear you go and help that nice boy at Stone House on certain days; so we won't interfere with that. But how about coming here every Monday, for a start?"

She stared at him. "Could I *really*? But—what did Dad say? Wouldn't—wouldn't it be too much bother for you?" she stammered.

"No bother at all; I wouldn't suggest it, if I wasn't interested in your work. And your father agrees, though he's trying to insist on paying me a fee! But I said we'd discuss that later, when we see how you get on. I could help you for a while, anyway, until you're old enough to think about getting into an Art School."

"An Art School? Do you really think I'd be good enough—to go in for it properly?"

"A good deal depends on whether you're prepared to work hard. If I give you an hour's coaching every week, I'll expect you to do a lot of home-work for me."

Joanna tried to thank him, then hurried off home, forgetting all about bicycles and fortunate children who had two sound legs apiece. She and her mother were still talking about the artist's wonderful offer when Mr. Wilson came home, and then the discussion started all over again. After a while, Joanna went up to her room to start on a new drawing. She planned to have a collection of drawings of different subjects ready for Mr. Mitchell to correct and advise on, at the first lesson.

"He thinks so highly of her work, he wants to teach her for nothing," her father said, when she had gone upstairs. "I said I couldn't allow that; if she's to have art lessons, I'll pay for them."

"I should think so!" agreed his wife. "Especially as the Mitchells are not at all well off."

"That's what I thought—only I didn't like to say so! But he persuaded me to let her go to him for a few trial lessons; and after that, we'll talk about it again."

Lessons with a real artist were certainly something to look forward to, and helped to take Joanna's mind off the fact that Heather seemed to have forgotten all the plans they had made before the bicycle came.

"Mum wants to know how many there'll be for tea, Saturday," Andrew said, when he and Joanna were milking the goats on Thursday evening. Joanna could deal with Mandy by herself, now, and Andrew had made a second milking-stool so that both goats could be milked at the same time.

"I don't think there'll be anyone—except me," she replied sadly. She had to repeat this, because Andrew thought he couldn't have understood the first time.

"But—didn't Heather say she'd be bringing quite a crowd, to learn how to follow a Scouts' trail?" he asked.

"That was before Heather got her bicycle," Joanna reminded him. "She doesn't seem to be a bit keen on tracking, nowadays; and you know what the others are! They won't care about it, if Heather isn't there."

There was a pause, while Andrew thought this over.

"Actually, it might be better to be on our own, the first time," he said then. "You'll be able to learn all the signs, and get some practice; then, if the others want to join in later on, you'll be able to help me teach them."

Privately, he was not sorry to have Joanna to himself for a while. It would have been fun to have had a party, and he liked Heather . . . nobody could help it. But both he and she were fond of organizing and taking the lead; and there were times when he felt that he and Joanna got on very well without her. Already his mind was busy, planning an afternoon's programme for the two of them alone, instead of for the half-dozen he had expected.

"You know the little stone bridge, near the village, where we first met?" he said now. "I'll wait for you there, after dinner on Saturday; and we'll look for tracks in the mud, where the birds go down to drink from the shallow part of the stream. Then I'll lay a Scouts' trail from there, and you can follow it."

There was a softness in the air on Saturday, like the very first hint of spring. When Joanna limped down the road, a thrush was singing his heart out in the elm-tree, hazel catkins swung like little banners in the breeze, and she saw the first colts-foot blooming by the roadside.

She was climbing the stile before crossing the fields to the stream, when Heather came tearing past on her bicycle. She slowed down when she saw Joanna, then got off, and wheeled her bicycle back to the stile.

"Where are you off to?" she asked.

"Andrew and I are going to look for tracks, down by the brook. Then I think we're going to have a sort of tracking game," Joanna replied, looking wistfully at the bicycle.

"I'm meeting Jill and Marion, and we're going on a long expedition . . . miles and miles!" Heather informed her. "I'll have to hurry, as I'm late already." Yet still she lingered, as if reluctant to leave the forlorn-looking figure on the stile. Some of the brightness seemed to have gone out of the day at the sight of her; and Heather suddenly remembered a half-promise she had made to join in the Saturday tracking game.

"I expect you'll have terrific fun," she said awkwardly. "I rather wish I was coming with you ... but Jill and Marion will be waiting. I'll tell you what: let's join up next Saturday, shall we?"

She mounted and set off again, turning to wave before she disappeared round the corner. Joanna waited till she was out of sight, then clambered down from the stile and plodded across the field.

Andrew was standing by the bridge, staring so intently at the water that he didn't see her till she touched his arm.

"You're looking a bit glum!" he remarked, after a swift glance at her face. "Anything the matter?"

"N-no—not really. It's only—I've just seen Heather going off for a bike-ride with some other girls ... and she stopped for a minute, and asked what we were going to do."

"Well? What's wrong with that?" he demanded.

"I knew she was only pretending to be interested, because she was sorry for me. I *hate* it when people do that ... and yet I'd have been crosser, I dare say, if she'd rushed past without stopping! I suppose I'm an idiot, really."

"You are, rather," he agreed cheerfully. "While those girls are careering along the roads, missing all the real fun, there are all sorts of exciting things for us to see here. If you'd come a few minutes earlier, you'd have seen a water-rat sunning himself on the bank there. He plopped into the water as you came up, and now he's swimming about. But you can see his head—look!" He pointed, and Joanna caught a glimpse of the top of a wet sleek head, before it disappeared among the water-weeds.

"And look here!" Andrew went on. "Where the bank shelves down gradually, there's a regular little beach of mud, simply covered with prints. This is where the water-rat went; and I think this must have been a moorhen."

There were the prints of several smaller birds as well; and Andrew suggested that she should make drawings of them in her book, while he laid the trail that she was to follow.

"You haven't shown me the Scout signs yet," she protested. "I shan't know what to look for, till you've taught them to me; and even then, I'm sure I'll never find them by myself."

"I'll lay a nice easy trail, this first time," he promised. "If you give me a good long start, I'll have time to make plenty of signs—so that you can't miss them."

He tied a knot in a tuft of grass, so that the ends leaned to one side. "That's one way of pointing the direction in which I've gone," he told her. Then he placed two stones one on top of the other, laying a third on the ground beside them. "If the third stone is on the right of the others, turn right; if it's on the left, turn to the left," he explained. "The two stones, one on top of the other without a third, means: 'This is the right trail; keep straight on'. When there are no stones or grass available, if I go through a wood, for instance, I'll lay pieces of stick in the shape of an arrow—like this. Or I might draw an arrow on the earth . . . but I don't do that too often, as it gives the show away to other people. It's far better to stick to our own special signs, if possible."

There was something rather thrilling in the idea of following a trail of secret signs, and Joanna soon lost her envy of the cycling party. Andrew explained that she need only look to the right, while following a path or going along a road, as Scout signs were always laid on the right-hand side. He took a stick and drew two other signs on the ground: an oblong with a number drawn inside and an arrow attached, for "letter hidden at so many paces in the direction in which the arrow is pointing"; a circle with a dot in the centre for "I have gone home".

"An X drawn on the ground, or formed by two sticks, means: 'This is *not* the trail'," he added. "And four stones in a row means the same thing. Now, get on with your sketching and don't look up; after ten minutes, you can begin to follow."

It took all of ten minutes to sketch the prints at the water's edge. She took special pains over them, so as not to be tempted to see where Andrew had gone. When the time was up, she tucked her sketchbook inside her coat, and searched the ground for the first sign.

A bunch of rushes knotted together showed that

Andrew had followed the course of the stream, and
a stone sign led her on in the same direction. A row
of four stones pulled her up short; but some knotted
grass indicated that she was to cross the brook which,
just there, was narrow enough to jump over.
Knotted grass on the opposite bank led her away
from the water to a little copse, where crossed
sticks showed that she must go no further in that
direction. True to his word, Andrew had laid the
trail especially clearly; and she found an arrow
made of three sticks without much difficulty.

Up a hill and down the other side; along a narrow
lane, over a bank and through another small copse,
she followed the trail made by grass, sticks and
stones, and an occasional arrow drawn in the mud.
She was a long way from the village, now, and she
guessed that Andrew was gradually heading towards his own home, and would end the trail with
the "I have gone home" sign.

She was climbing a wild, gorse-covered slope
when she first got into difficulties. She had covered
a lot of ground without seeing a sign, and guessed
that she must have missed one. Andrew had told
her that, if this happened, she must go back to the
last clue she had seen. There had been a stick arrow
near the hedge down below; and after returning to
it, she searched the ground round about in ever-
widening circles, till she found what she thought
must be the sign she had overlooked. Andrew had
filled his pockets with pebbles from beside the brook
—"In case I run out of material for clues," he had
explained. There were three flattish stones lying in

the grass at the foot of the slope. They were not arranged as a clue, and she realized that she must have walked over them without seeing them, and knocked them out of position. There was, therefore, no way of knowing in which direction the sign had pointed; so there was nothing for it but to "cast around" from that spot. This could have held her up for a long time; but looking for Scout signs had been good training in observation, and she soon caught sight of something that she would ordinarily have missed.

To the left of where the stones were lying, the grass was thin and poor, and in some places the bare earth showed through. And in one of these bare patches, there was an unmistakeable footprint. Having noticed this, she saw that the grass was slightly flattened as if it had recently been trodden down; and after that, it was a simple matter to find the next clue—some knotted grass—which led her up the slope at a different angle from that which she had first taken.

Having picked up the trail again, and feeling more confident from having surmounted a difficulty all by herself, she began to think that Andrew had been right in saying they would get on better without the others, this first time. It was easier to concentrate if one followed the trail alone; and she might never have seen the footprint if anyone else had been with her. At the same time, she was beginning to feel tired. The trail had led uphill for a long time; she was now on the high ground not far from Stone House; and she hoped it wouldn't be too long before she found the "I have gone home" sign.

If the rest of the trail were to lead more or less directly to Stone House, it would be downhill all the way; but a pair of sticks in the shape of an "X" showed that Andrew had turned aside, instead of making for home.

The next clues led her into a lane, bordered by tall hedgerows. She walked up and down it, vainly searching for stone or grass signs; then she stopped just in time to avoid treading on some marks drawn in the mud at the roadside. It was an oblong, enclosing the figure 6, and an arrow pointing down the lane. She took six paces, and found a folded piece of paper concealed under a stone on the grass verge.

With fingers which shook with excitement, she unfolded the paper. There was a faintly-pencilled message, made still more difficult to read by the smears of earth which covered it. But at last she managed to make out the words: "I AM GOING TO MEND HEATHER'S PUNCTURE. GO 50 PACES TO NORTH-NORTH-EAST THEN FOLLOW CART TRACK ON RIGHT TO HOUSE IN WOOD."

Chapter 11

THE HOUSE IN THE WOOD

SHE looked up and down the road, then read the message through again. She could see no sign of a house, and had no idea how to find north, south, east or west . . . to say nothing of north-north-east.

Then she remembered that the sun rose in the east and set in the west; but this didn't help her now, as the sky had clouded over and there was no sun to be seen. What a tease Andrew was, to write such a complicated message! Yet, if he had worded it more plainly someone else might have found it and followed him, and the whole point of this game was to keep the trail as secret as possible.

She gazed at the sky till her neck ached; and suddenly a brightness glowed through a gap in the clouds, just above the horizon to her left. So that must be the west; north, then would be straight ahead, and east to the right. If she took fifty paces up the road, veering slightly to the right . . .

Joanna paced it out; and, sure enough, there was a rough cart-track leading through a wood on the right of the lane. She set off down the track, feeling very puzzled by the message. It was natural that Andrew had stopped to help Heather, if he had found her with a punctured tyre. But why was it necessary to go to a house in the wood, in order to mend it?

Heather had asked the same question, after Andrew had found her disconsolately wheeling her bicycle along the lane. One of the tyres had gone flat soon after she had parted from her cousins, Jill and Marion; and as she had not bothered to learn how to mend a puncture, she was helpless till she met someone who knew what to do.

"Fancy taking your bike out before you've learnt to do your own repairs!" Andrew exclaimed scornfully.

"It's my own silly fault! I know that!" she agreed. "Daddy gave me a repair outfit, and wanted to show me how to mend punctures before I started, but I wouldn't wait. *Please*, Andrew, do it for me, just this once. Then I'll know how another time."

Andrew was already examining the outer tyre. "I can't find anything sticking into it," he muttered.

"I rode over some hedge-clippings a while back," she told him. "There were thorny twigs all over the road; I was on to them before I could stop. Could that have caused a puncture, d'you think?"

"Very likely. Did you notice a pool or a ditch with water in it, as you came along?" Then, as she shook her head, he said that they must wheel the bicycle to the nearest house, and ask for a bucket of water.

"That's to find the place where the tube is pierced," he explained, when she asked why he needed water. "There must be a house quite close by," he added, sniffing the air. "Can't you smell wood-smoke?"

He swung himself on to the lowest branch of a tree growing in the hedge, and began to climb. "It's over there, in the middle of that wood," he called down to her. "I can see the smoke from the chimney."

"What's happened to Jo?" Heather asked, when he had clambered down. "I thought you and she were playing a tracking game."

"I'll have to leave a message for her," he replied, fumbling in his pocket for a pencil and paper. Heather watched, fascinated, while he drew the secret sign and hid the letter.

"How is it that you know so many things?" she demanded, as they wheeled the bicycle along the cart-track through the wood.

"I don't really know much," he said, embarrassed and pleased at the same time. "I suppose, as I can't hear, I've had to rely on sight and smell more than other people do. And I've joined the Scout troop at school, and the Scouts' motto is 'Be Prepared'. All the tests and games are meant to teach us just that; to be ready for anything that might turn up."

There were many more questions Heather wanted to ask; but at that moment, they both came to a sudden standstill. The track had led them to a clear space in the middle of the wood, and in the clearing stood a little house.

"It must be the smallest house in the world!" whispered Heather. "I don't think I like it much; it's like a witch's house in a fairy-tale."

Andrew wasn't looking at her, so didn't hear what she had said. His eyes were on a rain-water butt at the corner of the house.

"There doesn't seem to be anyone about," he said.

"I don't suppose they'll mind if we use their water-butt for a moment."

"I think we ought to knock at the door and see if there *is* anyone at home," Heather protested.

He grinned at her. "Right-o! You go ahead and knock, while I take the inner tube out."

"We'll *both* knock," she said firmly. "I don't feel keen on going up to that door alone!"

They tapped softly at first, then beat a regular tattoo; but there was no answer. They turned away, both feeling more relieved than they cared to admit.

"Who on earth can be living in a place like this—right away from everywhere?" Heather wondered.

"A gamekeeper — or a woodman, perhaps." Andrew had turned the bicycle upside down, and was using a penny to lever off the outer tyre. "Whoever it is can't have gone far away . . . because I smelt something cooking!" He removed the inner tube and pumped some air into it. "Now for the water," he said, turning towards the butt. Heather suddenly grasped his arm and pointed towards the track by which they had come.

"There's someone coming!" she murmured. "A twig snapped . . . and—yes—I hear footsteps."

They both stared into the wood; then laughed with relief when Joanna appeared. Heather ran to meet her.

"Oh, Jo—I'm so glad it's you!" she exclaimed. "This place is giving me the pip! I keep expecting to see a witch, any minute!"

"You must have got on very well to have caught up so soon," remarked Andrew approvingly. He, too, was glad to see Joanna; not because he shared Heather's fancies, but because he had been a wee bit anxious about having left her to follow the trail alone. He had made the clues as obvious as possible, and didn't think she could have missed them; but this was the first time she had seen these signs, and he did not want her to spend the afternoon wandering miserably about by herself.

Now, satisfied that all was well, he returned to the business in hand. The girls watched while he held the partly-inflated tube under water, till tiny air-bubbles betrayed the damaged spot. Then taking each article as he needed it from Heather's repair-outfit, he sandpapered the place and covered it with a small patch of rubber, sticking it on with rubber-solution. He was pressing the patch tightly while the solution dried, when he noticed that the girls, who had stopped chattering, were looking nervous and uneasy. Following the direction in which they were staring, he saw a tall, thin woman with piercing black eyes and iron-grey hair. She was walking slowly towards them, and had evidently just emerged from the wood, as she carried a load of firewood in her apron.

She didn't look in the least annoyed, or even surprised, at seeing three children making themselves at home just outside her house; yet, without knowing exactly why, all three of them felt uneasy and longed to be somewhere else.

"I wish we hadn't come," muttered Joanna. "It isn't nice here . . . and how *are* we going to explain to her?"

Fortunately Heather remembered her manners, and went towards the woman, who had stopped to lay her sticks in one of the many untidy, broken-down sheds which surrounded the house.

"We're awfully sorry," Heather said. "And we do hope you don't mind us mending the puncture just here? We *did* knock at the door—but there was no one at home."

The woman gazed intently at each of them in turn; then she said: "You're welcome, I'm sure. And if there's anything you need, you have only to ask."

She spoke in a sort of whining drawl, and the girls instinctively moved nearer to Andrew, who was replacing the inner tube on the wheel.

"That's a fine new bicycle you have there," remarked the woman. "Which of you lucky young folks is the owner of it?"

The question was addressed to Andrew, and Heather had to explain that he was deaf . . . adding that the bicycle belonged to her. The black eyes rested on Andrew for a moment, then on Joanna's surgical boot.

"You'll be the young lady with the little dog," she said suddenly, turning to Heather.

"How *did* you know?" exclaimed Heather, wishing more than ever that they had never come to this queer place. The woman smiled mysteriously, and

Joanna nudged Andrew and asked him if he had nearly finished.

"It'll do, now, I think," he replied. He had got the outer tyre on, and was pumping it up.

"A pity you didn't wait till my son came home. He'd have fixed it for you with pleasure," the woman said. "I must go in, now, and see to his tea—so I'll say good afternoon to you."

They thanked her, and all heaved sighs of relief when she disappeared indoors.

"I *said* it was a witch's house!" Heather whispered, trying to laugh.

"Don't be such a baby!" snapped Joanna. "There aren't such things as witches. You know that quite well."

"She can't be an ordinary person," argued Heather. "She asked about Rory—as if she *knew* us; yet she'd never seen us before."

"If she goes down to the village shop, she might have seen you with Rory in the distance," Joanna suggested. "Or perhaps someone told her about you."

"She looks the sort of person who'd know things —without being told," Heather said slowly.

Joanna disliked this idea so much that she actually felt quite cross with Heather . . . also with Andrew, who had wandered off towards the sheds, looking for a piece of sacking to wipe his hands on. She ran after him and tugged at his arm.

"Do come away!" she said impatiently. "It's awfully rude to snoop about the place like this. And we want to go home."

"It may be rude, but sometimes it's necessary to do a bit of snooping!" he retorted. "Just take a look at what's in this outhouse!"

The floor of the shed was littered with an assortment of curious objects. Neither of the girls had seen anything like them before, but they knew at once that they must be traps of various kinds. There were steel gins for rabbits; and cages made of cunningly-woven hazel wands, to trap pheasants, Andrew explained in a whisper. And from a hook on the wall, hung a bunch of wire snares, like the one in which Rory had been caught.

"D'you think—do these belong to *her*?" whispered Joanna, glancing fearfully towards the house. "How dreadfully cruel she must be!"

"More likely they belong to that precious son of hers," Andrew replied. "Look here!" He stooped, and pointed to some large footprints in the mud near the entrance to the shed. "D'you remember that sketch you made, Jo?"

Joanna examined the pattern of the nails in the footprint, then clapped her hand over her mouth to suppress a squeal of excitement. "It *is*! It's the boy who trapped poor little Rory!" she gasped. "I remember where those nails were missing. I'm *sure* it's the same footprint."

"He must have described us to his mother, and that's how she knew about us," exclaimed Heather. "I'll never dare let Rory go outside the garden, with these frightful traps all over the place!"

"I hope they won't be all over the place much longer," Andrew said grimly. "I told the policeman about that snare we found, and he asked me to report straight to him if we saw any more."

He walked quickly across the clearing and along the path through the wood, forgetting to suit his pace to Joanna's, so that she had difficulty in keeping up with him.

Heather followed them, pushing the bicycle. "Don't look back," she muttered to Joanna. "I'm sure *she's* watching us from the window!"

When he reached the road, Andrew waited for them to come up.

"Jo is coming back to help me with the farm work, and staying to tea," he told Heather abruptly. "I suppose you wouldn't like to come too?"

"I'd love to," she replied. "I'd better dash home and ask Mummy first; but I'm sure she'll say yes— and I'll cycle straight over to Stone House. I'll be there nearly as soon as you are."

He hesitated a moment. "You'll pass the Police House on the way," he said then. "I'd meant to go there as soon as I've finished work; but meanwhile the poacher may have hidden his traps, if he suspects we've seen them. I think you'd better call in there now, and tell P.C. Hammond what we've found."

Chapter 12

SIGNS AND CLUES

WHEN Heather and Joanna came out of church with their parents on Sunday morning, they found Andrew waiting for them with the village constable.

"I want you three young folks to come along, and show me just where that puppy got caught in the snare," he said. "I won't keep you long; you'll be home in good time for dinner!"

On the way, he told them that he had written down Heather's report, but had been unable to go to the house in the wood until late in the evening. "And there wasn't a gin or a snare to be seen!" he said. "I might have thought you'd dreamt up the whole thing, if it wasn't that I happen to know something about the chap what lives there!"

"Who is he?" asked Andrew.

"His name's Joe Hawkins. I've had my eye on him for quite a while. He's half-gipsy; and he does no regular work, and no more does his ma. And what *I'd* like to know is—how do they make a living? Not by any honest means, I'll be bound."

They showed him the place where they had found Rory; but there was no snare there now.

"Poor little dog! He might have been killed," said Heather.

"It'll be all right now. Mr. Hammond will see that he doesn't set any more traps," Joanna consoled her.

"That's all very well, but I've not actually *seen* anything yet," said the constable. "It isn't that I doubt your word; but I've got to have proof before I can do something about it. Anyway, I'll keep a watch on that house; and maybe I'll find an excuse to make a search there."

After that, it was a rush to get home and have dinner before Sunday School started. Andrew had furthest to go, and when he reached Stone House it was time to set out again. But his mother had a cheese sandwich and a banana ready for him, and he ate them on the way to the Rectory.

All the children who had attended before were present; and seven more had come, having heard how much the others had enjoyed the class. After the opening hymn and prayer, Mrs. Fielding asked those who could remember to repeat the words: Show me thy ways . . . Lead me . . . Be thou my guide . . . and explained about "the Way" to the new ones.

"Now," she said, "we are going to try and learn about *how* God guides us and shows us what He wants us to do." She made them find the verse in Psalm 32:

"I will inform thee, and teach thee in the way in which thou shalt go: and I will guide thee with mine eye."

She asked them to imagine a great king with his servants waiting near him, all eager to obey his slightest wish. Only the most faithful and trusted servants would be near the king; and they would know him so well, and be so accustomed to studying his ways, it would not always be necessary for him to speak in order to let them know his will. A look would be sufficient.

"I want you to remember this," she said. "And to help you to do so, we are going to play a game! First—the two eldest must pick sides."

The two eldest were Heather and Sally; and when they had picked their sides, Mrs. Fielding said that Heather's side were to be her "servants".

"I want my servants to discover which object in the room I want brought to me—without the other side finding out first," she explained. Eighteen pairs of eyes were fixed intently on her face; but it was not easy to learn anything from her expression, as she had to guide her servants without betraying her thoughts to the other side. It was not long, however, before Andrew triumphantly seized a book which lay on the window-sill, and brought it to his mother who admitted that he had guessed right.

"Andrew was quickest that time," she said. "Because he knows me better than the rest of you do—so it's easier for him to interpret my thoughts and carry out my wishes. But although he knows me so well, he wouldn't have succeeded if he had not been watching me; if he had been thinking of other things instead of paying attention."

She asked them to read from Psalm 123: "Unto thee lift I up my eyes, O thou that dwellest in the heavens. Even as the eyes of servants look unto the hand of the master . . . even so do our eyes wait upon the Lord our God."

"First and foremost, you must be His servants," she told them. "To be His servant, means surrendering your whole life to God, so that you belong to Him in every way. Then, you must learn to know Him—through reading the Bible, and through trying to please Him. But even if you know Him, He cannot show you His will unless you are attentive, watchful, and ready for the least sign, like a faithful servant whose eyes are always on his Master."

"How can our eyes be on him when we can't see Him?" Peter demanded.

"If you love a person very much, more than anyone or anything else in the world, you will be thinking about him even if you cannot see him," was the reply. "Because you love him and want so much to please him, you will have learnt to know him. And you will often find that you are able to do what he wants, without having it put into words."

Peter still looked doubtful; so Mrs. Fielding asked them to look up one more verse, from St. Mark's Gospel.

"Thou shalt love the Lord thy God with all thy heart, and with all thy soul, and with all thy mind, and with all thy strength."

"This is what it is to be a Christian," she said. "You love Him with your whole heart; your soul—that is, your spirit, *wants* to serve Him; your mind is attentive to Him; and your strength is devoted to doing His will."

Heather asked Andrew and Joanna to come home with her for a few minutes, as there had been no time to talk over their interview with P.C. Hammond.

"I rather hated this morning," she confided to them. "I felt all excited and important, going to make that report yesterday. Yet afterwards, I rather wished I hadn't done it!"

"I know what you mean; it's horrid telling tales," Joanna agreed. "And somehow it seems worse, doing it on Sunday."

"I think that's silly," Andrew said decidedly. "You can't want Joe Hawkins to go on torturing animals with all those traps and snares. And the only way of stopping him was to go to the police."

"Anyway, it *hasn't* stopped him, yet," Joanna reminded them. "All we've done is to make him furious with us. When the policeman went there last night, Joe must have guessed it was our doing— if his mother told him we'd been there. And we've just made an enemy of him, without doing any good."

Andrew thought it was rather thrilling to have an enemy, and refused to share in her depression; and Heather had run on ahead to release Rory, who had started yelping as soon as he heard her footsteps.

"Come on in, and have a look at Daddy's picture," she suggested, when they caught her up. "It's a portrait of Mother; he was working on it all yesterday, and he wants to send it to an exhibition when it's finished."

Mr. Mitchell met them at the door, and willingly agreed to let them inspect the oil-painting which was propped on a chair in the living-room. It was unfinished, and Joanna was puzzled by it, even while she felt sure that it was going to be a very wonderful picture. To her eyes, it was—and was not —Heather's mother. It was as if the artist had seen through and beyond the hardworked wife and mother, to the young girl he had known long ago . . . and who was there still, behind the tired worn face and shabby clothes.

"I suppose that's how *he* sees her," Joanna thought, noticing that the artist had made no attempt to flatter, or make the face and hands look younger. Every line was there, every trace left by hard work and anxiety; but it was as if, like the faded blue overall, they were unimportant details.

"I'm glad you find it worth looking at!" Joanna swung round, startled, to meet the twinkling eyes of the artist who had been watching her as intently as she had been examining his painting. "Keep that dog away from the picture," he added to Heather, who, with Andrew, had been romping with the puppy.

"We don't want nasty oil-paint on your lovely coat, do we, pet?" she crooned, snatching Rory out of harm's way.

"I'm afraid I was thinking of my picture!" re-marked her father. "If he had collided with it, a little turps would get the paint off him in a moment; whereas I would have had several hours' work to repair."

"I know, Daddy! I was only teasing; we'll be careful, I promise," Heather assured him, trying to coax Rory to the other end of the room. Seeing that Joanna was genuinely interested, Mr. Mitchell went up to the tiny attic to fetch some more pictures for her to see. While he was out of the room, Heather's small brother, Simon, seized Joanna's hand, and persuaded her to join in the rough-and-tumble with the puppy. Like the others, she was on her hands and knees on the floor when Mr. Mitchell returned; but she got up at once when he came in, as she was really anxious to see the paintings.

"D'you know, I really think I'd better show these to you tomorrow, when you come for your lesson," he said, surveying the boisterous scene. "We'll banish Heather and her dog to the kitchen, then, and make sure of some peace and quiet!"

Even as he spoke, there was a sudden lull in the noise. Andrew had just noticed the time, and said that he ought to be going; and the puppy was whining to go out, so Heather let him into the garden. Seeing that the fun was over, Simon trotted off to the kitchen to find his mother, and Joanna helped Heather to collect the cushions and various oddments which were strewn about the floor. But Mr. Mitchell said no more about showing her his pictures, so Joanna concluded that he meant to wait till she came for her lesson, even though order had now been restored. She and Andrew had just said good-bye and were going through the door, when they heard an exclamation from Heather's father.

"Look here! This is really too bad," he was saying to Heather. "I told you to keep the puppy away from here, and now, see what he's done!"

"Oh Daddy—how simply awful! I *am* sorry!" Heather was looking at the smudged patch on the portrait with dismay. "But I really don't think it could have been Rory, this time; I didn't let him go to that side of the room, after you told me not to."

"He was all over the place, when I saw him," grumbled her father. "But then, so was Simon. It might just as well have been him, I suppose."

He called through to the kitchen to ask his wife whether there was any paint on Simon's hands or clothes; and Heather ran into the garden and grabbed Rory.

"There's not a spot of paint on his coat," she announced, returning with the puppy under her arm, just as Mrs. Mitchell called back that Simon was free from tell-tale marks.

"Yet it must have been one or the other," muttered the artist, still gazing sadly at the smudged painting. "Unless it was those cushions you were throwing about. . . ."

Andrew and Joanna had been waiting nervously, half in and half out of the door; but now, as there was nothing they could do, and neither had an idea of how the damage was done, it seemed best to slip quietly away.

Chapter 13

THE PAINT-MARK

AFTER tea Joanna's mother asked about the Sunday School, and listened with interest while Joanna described the game they had played to illustrate the verse: "I will guide thee with mine eye."

"Mrs. Fielding must be a wonderful teacher," she remarked, when she had heard the last part of the lesson—the explanation of "loving God with your whole heart".

"With your soul, you *want* to serve Him; with your mind, you are attentive to Him; and your strength is devoted to doing His will," Joanna's father repeated. "That's a grand definition of a Christian." He took Joanna's hand and drew her towards him. "Is that where you are now?" he asked her gently.

"I don't know . . . I *think* so. I *want* to," she murmured, staring at the floor.

"To want it: that's the first step," said Mr. Wilson. "Have you told Him this—and asked Him to accept you?"

"Well, yes, I asked Him today," she said shyly. "We knelt down at the end, and there was a prayer:

'Just as I am, I come to Thee this day
Through Jesus Christ our Lord, the only Way.'

And then there was a time for silent prayer: and I

98

asked Him to take me. But . . . I don't see . . . how can I *know*—when there isn't an answer?"

"The answer is given in advance," her father reminded her. " 'He that cometh unto Me, I will in no wise cast out.' Which is most likely to be true? God's word—or the silly doubts and fears put into your heart by Satan?"

"Well, of course—God wouldn't say something that wasn't true!" she said, her face brightening.

"Remember that! And 'Be not faithless, but believing'," said her father.

"It's a help to make a habit of remembering that you belong to God, first thing every morning," Mrs. Wilson added. "Ask Him to take charge of the day—and of all you think and do and say, and everything that happens. Then remind yourself, throughout the day, that He *is* in charge; that nothing can happen to you by accident."

It may have been because she knew her child so well that Mrs. Wilson hit on exactly the right words to give her the confidence and assurance she so badly needed. In a flash Joanna felt that she understood all she had ever heard and read, from the Bible and from certain hymns and psalms, about the joyfulness of those who trust in the Lord. The next morning, when she committed the day to God, she realized for the first time what it was to feel lighthearted and free from care.

"Don't rely on your own feelings, though," her mother warned her when she saw her off to school. "Just remember the *fact* that God is taking care of you, no matter what you feel like."

All the same, the feeling of happiness and of having made a new start continued all through the day at school. Lessons seemed more interesting; everyone she spoke to was in a friendly mood, and there was the drawing-lesson with Heather's father to look forward to when school was over.

"Did your father discover how the portrait got smudged?" she asked Heather during break.

"He hasn't said any more about it," replied Heather. "But I think he still suspects Rory—which is awfully unfair, as I'm sure the poor darling never went near it. Daddy was up very early this morning, scraping away with his palette-knife before re-painting it. The trouble is, he has so little time for his own work."

Joanna felt more grateful than ever to the artist for offering to teach her, and determined to do her very best. He had told her to come to his house straight from school, so as to make the most of the daylight. But Mrs. Wilson had insisted that Joanna was to come home first, and get clean and tidy before going to the Mitchells' house.

"Mr. Mitchell comes out from Northminister on the bus, and that's often a little late," she had said. "If you hurry, you'll probably get to his house no later than he does."

For all that, it was a nuisance having to go home first, and Joanna was in an agony of impatience while her mother brushed down her coat and then sent her back to the bathroom to remove an ink-stain from her finger.

"My hands will soon have paint all over them,"

she pointed out. "So why bother about a tiny ink-stain?"

"That reminds me—where did you go yesterday to get paint on your Sunday coat?" asked her mother. "It was oil-paint, too; I had to use turps to get it off."

"Oil-paint! On my coat?" Joanna's heart missed a beat, and she felt quite cold.

"Yes—a tiny smudge of blue paint. You must have brushed against something," Mrs. Wilson said. "I've got it clean now; but do be more careful when you've got your best clothes on."

All the way to the Mitchells' house, Joanna thought and thought of what she was going to say. She had been so certain that she had never touched the portrait. But now she remembered that she had unbuttoned her coat; and being loose, it must have swung out while she was romping with the puppy. Swung out, and brushed against the painting. And others were being blamed, perhaps, for something that she had done. No—not exactly blamed; but Simon had been suspected, and Mr. Mitchell had spoken quite sharply to Heather about keeping Rory under proper control.

"I'll see what happens when I get there," she thought. "If nobody says anything about it—and perhaps Mr. Mitchell will be able to make it just as good as it was before. . . ." But, deep in her heart, she knew she ought to tell about the patch on her coat. Yet—she hadn't actually seen it; she would never have known, if her mother hadn't mentioned it.

"If he says anything about it, then I'll tell him," she decided. "I'll wait—and see what happens."

As with most people who await a convenient opportunity for doing what they know to be right, no opening occurred for Joanna to make her confession. Mr. Mitchell banished Heather and Rory from the living-room, sat down at the table in a business-like way, and began looking through the drawings Joanna had brought. Some were coloured, and some in black-and-white; Joanna had worked hard at them, being anxious to make a good impression.

It may have been because she had studied so hard to make an impression, that most of these were less successful than the ones she had done to please herself—of which Mr. Mitchell had already seen samples. She was both astonished and disappointed when the artist finally picked out the three which she had considered the least successful, and tossed all the others aside as if they were not worth bothering about.

"These three have got something," he said abruptly. "Not much, it's true; but enough to work on. At least you were trying, with these, to capture what you actually *saw*. In the others," he carelessly flicked the discarded pile, "you were drawing what you thought you were *expected* to see."

"I don't know what you mean," she said, rather sulkily. "I always try and draw what I see."

She picked up the coloured sketch which had pleased her most: Andrew's geese with a sunny brick wall as background, and a holly-bush in the right-hand corner.

"Yes; that's an example of what I meant," said her teacher. "You were not really *seeing* that scene when you coloured it that way. You thought: White geese, green grass, red brick, dark-green leaves . . . and you painted them just so—like an advertisement for a soap-powder! But an advertising-poster is not a *picture*. Go and look at those geese again, and paint what you really see. I think you'll find that there are blue and grey shadows on them, and green reflected on their plumage; probably other colours as well, though the general effect may be white. And you will see that the bricks are not that flat red colour, but a mixture of many tints. Also, unless I am mistaken, the leaves will look more blue than green."

Joanna was by now thoroughly interested. "Goodness! How silly I am! I must have been blind," she exclaimed.

"If you realize that, then we have made a beginning," remarked the artist. "Now, today we will base our lesson on a discussion of these three that I have selected."

"I very nearly didn't bring those!" she confessed. "I had awful trouble with them."

"Yes; the subjects you chose were ambitious. And perhaps that is just why you forgot to be blind—and really saw what was before your eyes. Take this unfinished pencil sketch of the boy milking a goat. You didn't shut your eyes on the scene and draw *any* boy and *any* goat; you drew something which you saw happening at that particular moment. Consequently, you have made it live . . . although the proportions are wrong and the perspective is all over the place. But that is where I can help you."

An hour passed like a flash. Joanna could hardly believe her ears when Heather called from the kitchen that time was up, and would her father please come and have his tea.

"Mind you work hard, and bring me something good next week!" Mr. Mitchell said, getting up. His words came as a great relief to Joanna, as she had been afraid he would say that it was not worth going on with the lessons.

His criticisms had been a severe blow to her pride. Though she had lacked confidence in a general way, drawing was the one thing which she had thought she did really well. She didn't know, yet, that Mr. Mitchell was especially severe and strict with those pupils whom he thought most worth taking trouble over. But in spite of his severity, this first lesson had been an exciting experience, and she felt that she had been introduced to a new world.

She was half-way home before she remembered that she had said nothing about the damaged painting and the mark which had been found on her Sunday coat.

Chapter 14

FALSE TRAILS

UNTIL quite recently, Joanna had been accustomed to find the time hang heavily on her hands.

During this week, however, it was difficult for her to fit in all she wanted to do; or rather, to do what she wanted, as well as the things other people expected of her. After her lesson with Mr. Mitchell, she grudged every moment that was not spent drawing and painting. School was a nuisance; the jobs she was expected to do at home, even more so. And she cut short her time at Stone House on Tuesday and Thursday, because she wanted to get home and go on with her painting.

"What's the matter?" Andrew asked. "Are you tired of farm work already?"

"No, of course not. I love it, really," she replied. "It's just that there's so little free time—and it's a puzzle to know what to put first."

"I think you're being rather selfish," her mother said, when for the second time Joanna came home early, leaving Andrew to finish the work alone. "You were glad enough to help him when you'd nothing better to do. It's not like you to keep taking things up and then dropping them."

"I *don't* do that; at least, I don't mean to,"

sighed Joanna. "But there seems so much going on, these days, I'm all in a muddle."

"I suppose we've only ourselves to blame," her mother murmured half to herself. "We used to worry so about you, and we were always trying to find something to make you happy and keep you amused; it's no wonder if you're self-centred."

Joanna pretended not to hear this; but her cheeks burned as she bent over the drawing which would *not* come as she wanted it. "Even this is going all wrong now," she muttered, throwing down her pencil in despair.

"You've been doing too much of it," her mother said. "You're getting stale, I expect."

"Mr. Mitchell said I was to work hard at it," Joanna protested.

"You can work hard at something, without letting everything else go," Mrs. Wilson told her. "I notice you've even been cutting short your Bible-reading and prayers, so it's not surprising that your life's all wrong."

Joanna got up and went quickly out of the room. She didn't want to admit that her mother had touched on the real heart of the trouble—which was that she was finding it quite impossible to say her prayers at all. She had tried; but it was as if she had lost the way somewhere, like that time when she had missed one of Andrew's clues in the tracking game. Her life *was* all wrong; she was, as she had said, "In a muddle". And it was partly to stop herself from thinking about it that she was working so hard at her drawing and painting.

At school, during break, Heather asked if she and Andrew were going to have another tracking game on Saturday.

"I want to come and learn how to make those Scout signs," she said.

"I don't know if I'll have time to go to Stone House," Joanna said shortly. "I've something I want to finish before my next lesson with your father. And anyway, I thought you'd be going for a bike-ride, like you did last Saturday."

Heather said no more, but she thought a great deal. She had had a guilty conscience about having disappointed Joanna the week before; and she guessed that Andrew must be feeling lonely and neglected, now that Joanna, in her turn, had found an absorbing occupation. She cycled over to Stone House early on Saturday, and found Andrew cleaning out the henhouses by himself. After helping him for a while, she asked if she could come again in the afternoon and learn to make the tracking signs.

"I don't know if Jo's coming," he replied gloomily. "She's so taken up with her drawing, these days, she's got no time for anything else."

"We needn't be more than two to play it, though, need we?" she asked.

"Well, no; it's better, in a way, with only two," he agreed. "Jo and I had a lot of fun last time, with one laying the trail and the other following."

He began to show her the Scout signs, and Heather did some more thinking. Then she said, rather shyly:

"If I can persuade Jo to come over after dinner,

would you care to borrow my bike and go for a ride
—while she and I practise tracking? Then we'd
both help you with the farm work."

His face lit up at the suggestion of a bicycle ride;
and though he hesitated to accept her offer, as the
bicycle was still so new and precious, it did not
take Heather long to persuade him.

She secured Joanna's co-operation by the simple
method of going to her house after dinner, and
telling her to "Come along!" By this time Joanna
was quite relieved to have someone else to make
decisions for her; and they walked to Stone House
together, Heather pushing the bicycle.

"Now, you'd better lay the trail, Jo, as you've
played before; and I'll follow," Heather announced, when they had arrived. "I'm lending
Andrew my bike for the afternoon."

"I'll be back in an hour," he promised. "And if
neither of you has turned up by then, I'll come and
look for you."

It took far longer to make the signs than Joanna
had expected, and she was glad that Heather was
giving her a good start. She became quicker at it
after a while, and by the end of half an hour found
herself quite a long way from Stone House. She
made a wide turn, then, preparing to come back
by a roundabout way. She was crossing a stretch of
heathland, making grass signs from time to time,
when to her amazement she saw Heather coming
towards her.

"What are you doing? You're right off the trail!"
she shouted.

"No, I'm not; I've been following the signs all the way," Heather retorted, running up to her. "Look here!" She returned on her tracks with Joanna following her, and pointed to a stick arrow, the last clue she had seen.

"But—I never made that sign," Joanna protested. "There must be other people playing the same game, and our lines got crossed."

"I say—that's rather fun," Heather said. "Perhaps they are real Scouts. Let's follow *their* trail and see what happens at the end."

The strange trail crossed the heath at right-angles to the route Joanna had meant to take, and led them still further away from Stone House.

"We'll be late getting back, if it goes on much longer," Joanna said. "I wonder if we ought to give up?"

"There's a by-road ahead; let's go that far, and see which way it leads us from there," Heather suggested.

"Some of these clues are awfully bad—hardly Scout signs at all," complained Joanna. "They can't have been made by real Scouts."

"I liked what Andrew's mother said about Christians following step by step—just like this," remarked Heather. "I think some of the things she tells us are a terrific help, don't you?"

"Well—yes; I *did* think so, at first. But now—I'm all mixed up, somehow. I seem to have got out of touch, and I just don't now what to do about it," Joanna said despairingly.

Heather hesitated; then she said: "D'you

remember Mrs. Fielding saying that sometimes we
get lost because we've sort of missed a sign . . .
missed something God wanted us to do; and that
we can't get anywhere till we've gone back and put
it right? D'you suppose that could be the trouble—
with you?"

"Y-yes; I think it could," Joanna said slowly.
"Stop here a minute, while I think."

Heather waited, distressed by her friend's unhappy face.

Joanna hadn't really needed to think of what the
missed sign had been; she knew, only too well, and
was merely trying to summon enough courage to
make her confession to Heather. "It was something
I ought to have owned up to—and didn't," she said
at last. And then she told Heather about the paint-
mark which had been found on her coat, and of how
she had shirked owning up to Mr. Mitchell.
"Everything's gone wrong since then," she ended
miserably."

"Poor old Jo! It must have been horrid for you,"
Heather sympathized. "I know you'd have owned
up at once, if you'd seen it at the time. But finding
out afterwards must have made it that much more
difficult."

"It'll be a whole lot worse, telling him, after
putting it off so long," Joanna said tearfully.

"Let's go home now, and tell him straight away,"
Heather suggested in her usual decided manner.
"Then we can forget all about it, and come back and
help Andrew. He won't mind if we're a bit late."

A quick glance round showed them that their

best way was to get on to the by-road which lay ahead of them; and they made their way towards it, still following the strange trail.

"Look, Heather! There's a 'letter hidden' sign, by the roadside." shouted Joanna. "Five paces in this direction . . . quick! Let's find it and see what it says."

"Perhaps we shouldn't—if it isn't meant for us," Heather objected.

"Oh bother! I suppose we ought to leave it, then. And it may have been found already, by whoever was following. Though Andrew said Scouts are supposed to destroy all clues as they find them. We only left them last time, in case I got lost and had to go over them again."

"I'm wondering . . . I suppose it's just possible that this trail *was* laid for us," Heather said slowly. "Andrew might have done it, as a joke, and the letter would explain it. Perhaps—it would be all right to look at it—just to see?"

They were both longing to read the letter; and now Joanna settled the question by lifting the stone under which it had been concealed.

The message was written in red pencil and in large capital letters; and after reading it, they stared at each other in silence.

"It *can't* be for us!" Heather said at last. "Who—how could it be—what do you suppose it means?"

This was what was written on the hidden letter:

"So you'd tell on me to the police, would you, you little sneaks. But I'll get even with you. Just see if I don't."

Chapter 15

"THE BICYCLE HAS GONE!"

MR. MITCHELL stood before his easel, his palette on his arm and a paintbrush in his hand. But he stopped working on the portrait in order to listen to Joanna's confession. When she had finished, he said: "Thank you for telling me. You did very little damage, and it hasn't taken long to put it right. But I can understand how you felt about it, and I'm glad, for your sake, that you've got it off your mind."

"She's been so miserable, Daddy," Heather put in. "It's a shame, really, because it wasn't in the least her fault."

"I don't think I'd have dared to own up, even now, if you hadn't come with me," Joanna told her.

"You'd have owned up, all right! Because you couldn't have gone on like that . . . not being able to pray, and feeling lost—and sort of out of touch with God," Heather reminded her.

Mr. Mitchell turned from his painting to look at the two girls. "So you've learnt that, have you?" he said. "That when God seems to have left us, it's really our own wrong-doing which is separating us from Him. He is there, all the time . . . just as the sun is always there, though clouds may separate us from its warmth and light."

His last words were nearly drowned by a violent knocking at the door. Heather went to open it, and Andrew burst into the room—so breathless, that he could hardly speak.

"It's gone! The bike's gone!" he panted. "I left it . . . leaning against a gate . . . when I was trying to find you—and to warn you about the false trail. When . . . I got back . . . it had disappeared."

"We must tell the police," Mr. Mitchell said quickly. "I'll go myself—then I can give him a complete description of the bicycle. You'd better come too, Andrew, and tell him exactly where you left it."

He was pulling off the overalls which he wore over his ordinary clothes while he was painting; and now he put on his coat and left the house, followed by Andrew and the girls.

"I'm frightfully sorry, Heather," Andrew said wretchedly, as they hurried down the road. "I ought to be shot for leaving it, even for a few minutes. But I'm going to try and find out who took it, and get it back—if it's the last thing I do!"

"Don't you worry. It's sure to be found soon," Heather said, speaking more hopefully than she felt, because she wanted to spare his feelings.

"What did you mean when you said you were trying to warn us of the false trail?" Joanna asked.

"I'd been going up hill; and stopped at a place where there was a good view of the countryside," he said. "And I saw you, Joanna, crossing a field; or rather, I guessed it was you; all I could see was a figure moving—and stopping every few yards, as

8

if to make the signs. I thought it would be rather fun to wait till Heather came in sight, and watch her pick up the trail. I expected to have to wait some time; but the first figure was hardly out of sight when I saw someone following . . . and I couldn't think how Heather could have got there so quickly. Then—whoever it was branched off in another direction . . . stopping from time to time, as though laying a new set of tracks. So I guessed someone was monkeying about with your trail, and cycled as fast as I could to what seemed the nearest point to that place—so as to intercept Heather, and warn her. I propped the bike against an open gate, and went into the field; and when I found the trail, I began to follow it *backwards*, hoping to meet Heather."

"I expect I'd got there before you, and started following the false trail," Heather said.

"Yes; that's how I missed you. I realized that, after a while, and went back to where I'd left the bike. When I found it had gone, I thought you might have taken it yourself, so I came straight here."

"Did you look for footprints, near where the bike had been?" Joanna asked, knowing that the question was unnecessary since he would certainly have done so.

"Of course I looked, but there was nothing very clear. I thought . . . but it's easy to imagine things."

"What did you think you saw?" demanded Heather.

"It was muddy near the gate; but there's been a herd of cows through there, and it wasn't possible to make out a complete footprint. But—I saw some that *could* have belonged to Joe Hawkins, the man who has all those traps, at the house in the wood. Have you still got that sketch you drew of his footprint, Jo?"

Joanna fished in her coat pocket for the sketch; and at the same time, Heather pulled a piece of paper out of her own pocket, exclaiming: "What an idiot I am! I quite forgot!" And she showed Andrew the threatening "hidden letter" they had found, while following the false trail.

Meanwhile, they had arrived at the door of the Police House, where Mr. Mitchell was already talking to P.C. Hammond. After answering the constable's queries about time and place, Andrew handed over the letter, while Heather explained how and where they had found it.

"If it was meant for you, then it seems like it must have been Joe Hawkins who left it for you, after trying to spoil your tracking game," the policeman said. "Though this isn't what I'd call evidence; not by a long way. He *might* have written that letter, just to give you a fright . . . and then seen his chance to pinch the bike, when he was on his way home. But then, anyone else might have pinched it, when all's said and done. If we can find him with the bike, that'll be another matter. I suppose you couldn't describe the chap who you saw laying the false trail?" he added, turning to Andrew.

"No, it was too far away," Andrew replied. "Actually, I thought it was Heather, at first . . .

though I remember thinking the person looked rather too tall to be her. But I wasn't even near enough to see if it was a man."

"Could you find an excuse to make another search at that house in the wood?" asked Mr. Mitchell.

"Yes, I can do that; I'll go along there now," said the policeman. "And I'll call in at yours on the way back, and tell the young lady if there's any news. But I'll be surprised if I find the bike there. Joe Hawkins wasn't born yesterday!"

There seemed nothing more to be done, for the present. Andrew told Heather again how dreadfully sorry he was, and she repeated her assurance that the bicycle was sure to turn up, sooner or later. Then she went home with her father, to wait for whatever news P.C. Hammond might bring.

As soon as they were out of earshot, Andrew said:

"I say, Jo, do you think you could manage the farm work by yourself? The milking can wait till I get there if you'd do the feeding, and shut up the poultry for me."

"I could try," she said doubtfully. "I'd be afraid of not doing it right, though."

"Ask Mum to help you," he said. "And tell her what's happened, and that I'm taking the next bus to Northminster. You see—I'm pretty certain Joe won't have taken the bike home. It would be too risky, since the policeman's got his eye on him already. It's more likely that he'll try to sell it, straight off; and as it's Saturday, he'd have to do it at once. Now, my guess is that he's ridden it straight to Northminster; and I want to look round every garage and cycle-repair shop, and all the places where they deal in second-hand goods before they close down for the week-end."

"Oh Andrew—how thrilling! But couldn't I come with you?" she begged.

"Someone *must* see to the animals and poultry," he said. "I'm awfully sorry; I know it's a lot to ask of you, Jo. But I can't carry this through unless you'll help me out at home."

Joanna hesitated. She didn't welcome the thought of trudging all the way to Stone House, with the alarming prospect of doing the farm work single-handed, before walking home again. And meanwhile Andrew would have all the excitement of tracking down the thief, and perhaps of returning in triumph with the bicycle. But then she remembered how her heart had ached for him in his deep distress at having lost Heather's bicycle; and she knew she must do what she could to help him.

"Right-o! I'll go and start now," she said, and was turning away without making any more fuss about it. But Andrew caught hold of her hand, and gave it a terrific squeeze, to show that he knew exactly how she felt.

Mrs. Fielding had given up expecting them back for tea, and had returned to her typewriter. But she told Joanna to call her if she was in difficulties, and promised to come out as soon as she had finished what she was doing. Joanna had by now become quite used to dealing with the poultry while Andrew milked the goats. But this evening they were unusually wild, and she had a lot of trouble getting them into their houses. Fortunately Mrs. Fielding came out to help, just as the bantams had flown over the fence into the garden.

"I've never known them like this before," Joanna complained. "I believe they're doing it on purpose!" Between them, they managed to get everything shut in safely; and then they collected the eggs.

"I haven't dared let the pigs out," Joanna said. "I just fed them in their sty."

"It won't matter for once," Mrs. Fielding assured her, "and I think we'd better leave the goats for Andrew to deal with."

"I'd like to milk Mandy," Joanna said, "she's always quite good with me, if you'll help me get her into the shed. Then Andrew will only have Milly to do, when he comes home."

At this very moment, Andrew was in a little cycle-repair shop in a back street in Northminster, asking if there was a second-hand bicycle for sale. This was the fifth shop he had tried; and by now he had learnt that it was better not to say straight out what he had come for. The smaller the business, the more guarded the proprietor became at the mention of stolen goods. So he said that he was looking for a ladies' bicycle for a friend; and having satisfied himself that Heather's was not there, he asked the man if he knew of any other place where he might find what he wanted.

"There's Stimson's, down by the river," the man said doubtfully. "His yard's a regular scrap-heap of old cars and spare parts; but now and then he has a push-bike in fairly good condition. I'd try there, if I were you."

The shops stayed open late on Saturdays, but they were all closing down as Andrew made his way through the poorer part of the town towards the river. When at last he found Stimson's, he didn't think it looked very promising. The yard was a regular "home for incurables". It seemed doubtful whether a whole car or motor-bike could have been made from the collection of wrecked vehicles assembled there. Mr. Stimson himself was not inclined to be helpful, either, being on the point of locking up and going home. But when Andrew pretended that he was prepared to pay a good price, he consented to show him a lady's bicycle—"almost new, which came in a week or two ago".

Andrew felt sure that the man was not speaking the truth; and he was even more sure of this when the bicycle was produced. It was certainly Heather's bicycle; and while Andrew pretended to haggle about the price, he was racking his brains to find a way of opening the tool-bag without arousing suspicion. He knew that Heather had had her name stamped on the metal label from a slot-machine, meaning to attach it to the bicycle. But having been, as usual, in too much of a hurry to fix it on, she had slipped it in among the tools—and then forgotten all about it. But Andrew remembered seeing it there when he had mended her puncture; and now, as Mr. Stimson refused to leave him alone for a moment, he said he wanted to make sure that the tool outfit was complete.

A quick glance was enough to see that this proof of ownership was still there; and he then said that he must consult his friend about the price. Since the business would be closed till Monday, there was no difficulty in persuading the proprietor to reserve the bicycle till then; and having settled this, Andrew went to the police station and asked the sergeant there to ring up Andrew's "friend"—P.C. Hammond.

Chapter 16

THE YOUNGEST KNIGHT

JOANNA had returned home feeling very tired, but happy at having done some "real work", very nearly on her own. She had a great deal to tell her parents, who knew nothing of the afternoon's adventures, but she said very little about her own doings. Looking after Andrew's farm for him, seemed unimportant and rather dull compared with having a bicycle stolen, and searching for it in a big town like Northminster. She still wished that she could have gone with Andrew on this exciting expedition; but it was impossible to feel discontented in the glow of peaceful happiness which had come to her after making her confession to Mr. Mitchell. She told her parents about this, too; and she had barely finished when there was a vigorous knocking on the door. Mr. Wilson opened it, and Heather burst into the room.

"It's been found! Andrew has found the bicycle!" she shrieked, while her father followed her through the door, apologizing to Joanna's parents for the intrusion.

"When this girl of mine gets the bit between her teeth, there's no holding her!" he explained. "And I can only hope you'll excuse us."

Mrs. Wilson asked him to sit down, and made

tea for everyone, while Heather poured out the story: How the constable had come to report that no bicycle had been found at the house in the wood; and how he had returned later to tell them of the telephone-call from Northminster.

"The police there will see that you get your bicycle back all right," P.C. Hammond had told Heather. "And now I'm off to have a few words with Mister Joe Hawkins! Young Andrew said how he'd got proof that the bike's yours. That's a real smart lad —and I wish we had more like him in the Force!"

The Mitchells had stayed at home, waiting till the next bus came in; and, as they had expected, Andrew came straight to their house to give them his own account of the discovery.

"Wasn't it brilliant of him?" Heather asked Joanna. "And fancy remembering where I'd put the label with my name on . . . when I'd forgotten all about it myself!"

"Hammond said that naturally the thief would have removed any visible identification-marks," added her father. "But he never thought of looking in the tool-bag!"

"And I'd nearly forgotten what we've come here for!" exclaimed Heather. "We really came to say —Three cheers for Jo! Andrew told us that, while he was having all the fun of the sleuthing, *you* stayed at home and took over all the dull hard work for him. He said you'd been an absolute brick, and that you deserved a medal!"

Joanna's father and mother looked at her inquiringly.

"What's all this? You didn't tell us you'd done anything special," Mrs. Wilson said.

"It wasn't anything special . . . only the ordinary farm work I sometimes help Andrew with," she mumbled. "And Mrs. Fielding had to come and help me, in the end."

"I like the way she says *only* the ordinary farm work!" laughed Heather. "I couldn't have taken that on alone to save my life!"

"I agree with Heather; it's Joanna who comes out top in this adventure," said Mr. Mitchell. "She reminds me of the story of the youngest knight, who was left alone to guard the castle while his brothers had all the excitement of the battle."

"I remember that old tale," Mrs. Wilson said, putting her arm round Joanna. "I used to think it was a good way of showing that it sometimes takes the most courage to do the out-of-sight work in the background."

"There was to be a gold star on the shield of the knight who had acquitted himself most bravely and faithfully throughout the battle," Mr. Mitchell went on. "And at the end of the day, the star was found on the shield of the youngest knight."